Thirteen Jars

J.D. Toepfer

CHAPTER 1 — THE WILDERNESS

Spotsylvania County, Virginia — May 1864

By the time darkness settled over the Wilderness, the battle had ended in name only, leaving the living to crawl from among the dead while the forest continued its slow, merciless burn.

The night air was thick with smoke, screams, and the sickly-sweet stench of charred flesh from men who would never rise again. At the time, it would have been easy to believe this was the end of it.

Fire crept through the undergrowth like slow, deliberate fingers, feeding on dry leaves, splintered trees, and brush dislodged by the fighting. The flames glowed low and hungry, igniting scraps of blue and gray cloth while licking at cartridge pouches, haversacks, and bodies that lay where they had fallen. Smoke drifted upward, turning the moonlight into a pale, sickly haze.

Somewhere in the distance, a musket cracked. Then another. Not volleys, but isolated shots, fired without purpose. It was as if the night itself twitched in a restless sleep. The cries of the wounded rose and fell in uneven waves. Some pleaded for water. Others for their mothers. A few screamed until their voices failed, leaving only hoarse gasps that echoed in their wounded chests.

Those who could still move dragged themselves across the ground, clawing at dirt and roots in desperate attempts to escape the creeping fire. Mangled limbs bent where they should not. Blood soaked into soil already blackened by the heat. Every bush seemed dressed in shreds of cloth, dark and stiff, fluttering faintly in the heated air like hideous banners.

Granville Smith Crockett lay on his back in a small clearing just off a narrow path, the ground beneath him uneven and hard. The pain in his chest had dulled to something heavy, like a great weight pressing him into the ground. Each breath came shallow and wet, accompanied by a soft, bubbling sound. When he lifted his head slightly, the effort sent a sharp spike of agony through him, and he let it fall back with a groan.

The moon hung above the tree line, round and uncaring, its light catching on the brass buttons of his blue coat and the dark, spreading stain that soaked through the fabric. He pressed his hand to his chest without thinking; his fingers grew slick instantly. When he brought them toward his face, they gleamed black in the moonlight.

Blood.

He tried to swallow, but his throat was dry, his tongue thick and useless. He would have given anything for water. Anything at all.

His brother lay at his feet.

Ridgely Smith Crockett lay on his side, one arm twisted beneath him at an unnatural angle, his face turned toward Granville as if he were merely resting. His eyes were open, glassy and fixed. The lower half of his gray jacket was burned away, revealing scorched, blackened flesh. Granville could still feel the weight of Ridgely's head where it had rested on his leg only moments before; he could still feel the sudden slackness and the dull thud as it dropped.

They had been speaking. Arguing, just as they had four years earlier.

Granville remembered Ridgely's voice raised above the din of battle, sharp with anger and something else; fear, perhaps, or regret. He remembered the words, though they now came in fragments, like scraps of paper torn loose and carried off by the smoke.

You didn't have to fight, Gran.
Against your own kin.
Now, this war's gonna swallow you whole.

Ridgely had always spoken as if he already knew how things would end.

Granville had not answered him. There had been no time. A roar like thunder, the sensation of being struck hard in the chest, and the sudden taste of iron in his mouth. Then the ground rushed up to meet him.

Now, Ridgely did not speak at all.

Granville stared at his brother's face, searching for a sign he knew would not be there. Breath. Movement. Anything. His chest tightened, not with pain this time, but with a slow, creeping certainty.

His brother was dead.

The knowledge settled over Granville like the ash falling from the air, quiet, but inescapable. He had known, of course. Had felt it in the slackening of Ridgely's weight. Still, seeing him like this, his eyes wide open, mouth slightly parted, made something inside Granville break loose.

"I'm sorry," he whispered, though he was not sure what for. For the argument. For surviving this long. For lying here while Ridgely lay dead at his feet.

The words came out thin and broken, barely louder than the nearby crackle of fire.

A sudden flare of heat washed over him as a line of flame crept closer through the grass. Granville tried to move his legs, but they responded only with a weak twitch. Panic rose in his throat, sharp and sudden.

Hell, he thought dimly. I am in hell.

The war had been spoken of in grand terms when it began: duty, honor, preservation, union. Sermons and speeches, with flags waving beneath clear skies. No one had spoken of this. Of men burning where they lay. Of forests turned into furnaces. Of brothers dying at one another's feet, wearing different colors.

War did not kill them all at once. It lingered, choosing who would be allowed to suffer longer.

The cries around him seemed to grow more distant, as if carried away by the smoke. The fire's heat no longer felt immediate. Even the pain in his chest began to fade, replaced by a deep, numbing cold creeping into his limbs.

Granville's breathing slowed. Each inhale took more effort than the last.

That was when he saw her.

At first, he thought she was a nurse, one of the women who sometimes ventured onto the field after the battle, risking death to tend the wounded. The figure moved with purpose, gliding rather than walking, her pale form catching moonlight as she passed among the bodies. She wore a dress, the common kind worn by women in the towns they endlessly marched through, though the details refused to settle clearly in his mind. Smoke curled around her, parted, and closed again without clinging.

She did not hurry. She did not hesitate.

Granville tried to call out, but his voice failed him. The sound died in his throat, little more than a rasp. Still, the figure turned her head slightly, as if she had heard something, all the same.

She drew nearer.

The air around her felt cooler, the smoke thinning as she passed. Moonlight clung to her in a way it did not to anything else, outlining her shape in pale silver. Granville could not make out her face, only the suggestion of eyes, dark and intent, fixed on the ground before her.

She stopped beside Ridgely.

Granville watched as she looked down at his brother, her head tilting as if in recognition. For a moment, a weak hope flared in his chest. Perhaps she would tend to him. Perhaps he was not dead after all.

Then she spoke.

Though the battlefield was anything but quiet, her voice carried clearly. It was calm and steady, composed despite the chaos around them. Still, the words were slurred, thinned by distance, by smoke, and the roar in Granville's ears.

"Your time has come," she said. "Are you prepared to go with me, Ridgely Smith Crockett?"

Granville's heart stuttered.

4

The name echoed strangely in his mind, the first part lost amid the ringing in his ears. He caught only the end—*Smith Crockett*—and the certainty that the words were meant for him.

He tried to turn his head fully toward her, but his neck would not cooperate. Panic stirred again, though it was weaker now, dulled by exhaustion and the creeping cold.

An angel, he thought.

The idea came without reason, settling easily into place. What else could she be? She glowed beneath the moon. She moved untouched through fire and smoke. Her voice carried peace in a place that had known nothing but violence.

Granville's lips trembled. He wanted to ask where she would take him, whether Ridgely would be there, and if it would stop hurting.

He could not form the words.

The figure remained still, patient, waiting. The nearby fire crackled, sending up a shower of sparks that faded before reaching her.

Granville drew in one last shuddering breath. His chest burned, then went oddly numb. The world narrowed to the pale shape before him and to the certainty that there was nothing left for him here.

No one had warned him that some questions were not meant to be answered.

"Yesssssssssssss," he whispered.

The word left his mouth as his breath did, thin and drawn-out, stretched by the fading strength in his lungs. It was little more than a sigh.

The figure inclined its head.

Granville's eyes closed.

For a time, how long he could not have said, there was nothing.

No fire. No pain. No sound.

The battlefield fell away entirely, leaving a vast, empty stillness. Cold pressed in on him from all sides, deep and absolute. Even the memory of warmth felt distant, unreal.

Then, without warning, air rushed violently into his chest.

Granville's body jerked, his back arching as he drew a great, desperate gasp. Pain tore through him anew, sharp and searing, and he cried out hoarsely as breath returned to lungs that had been still.

The world came crashing back.

Smoke burned his eyes. Fire crackled nearby. The screams of the wounded surged around him once more. His chest heaved as he dragged in breath after breath, each one ragged and raw.

He was alive.

The knowledge struck him with a force almost as great as the pain. His hands shook as he pressed them to his chest again, half-expecting to find nothing there. Blood still soaked his uniform. The wound still burned. Nothing had changed.

And yet…

Something was wrong.

Granville lay gasping beneath the moon. Staring up at the smoke-choked sky, a cold certainty was settling over him. Death had claimed him once already, and now whatever had answered his "*Yes*" had not finished with him yet.

The fire crept closer.

Somewhere nearby, something moved silently through the smoke, unseen but no longer distant.

CHAPTER 2 — THE GREAT RECESSION

Culpeper County, Virginia — Fall, 1920

The heat baked the dirt road, the air shimmering like a mirage. Not a breath of wind stirred the cornfields of old man Taylor's farm, their stalks bowed and yellowing before their time. The Gatlin brothers lingered on the porch of the Last Stop General Store, their boots scuffing dust into slow clouds, tobacco bulging in their cheeks.

"Ain't just the crops," the oldest brother, Eli, muttered, leaning back against the railing. "Whole damn world's going to hell."

"Men don't know what to do once the shootin' stops," he said. "Over there, you were told where to stand and who to kill. Here, you just watch things rot and get told to be grateful you're alive."

Eli stared at the statue honoring Confederate soldiers in the square. "Men came home from France thinkin' it'd mean somethin'. Turns out it don't."

He spat. The dark streak hit the ground with a wet thud and stayed there.

"Worthless," he muttered, squinting toward the fields. "Whole damn season ain't worth the sweat."

Beyond the withered fields, a white house stood untouched by drought, its fence straight, its white paint unblemished.

The middle brother, Calvin, chewed thoughtfully. "Costs more to haul it than it sells for. Pa would've let it rot."

"Pa's lucky he didn't live through the flu," Eli said. "Didn't have to watch folks cough themselves inside out. Didn't bury the neighbors two days apart."

Didn't have to walk a mile begging for help and come home wheezing, either—but Eli kept that thought to himself.

The youngest, Thomas, said nothing. He stood apart from them, hat brim low, eyes watching a grasshopper hopping in crooked arcs across the road. The insect landed on the store's steps, legs trembling.

Grace Wright stepped out the door, wiping her hands on her apron. Sixty-some years had etched lines into her face like the rocky crevices of the Blue Ridge Mountains, but her eyes were sharp. She gave the brothers a look that carried no fear and even less patience.

"You boys planning to buy something," she said, "or just poison my porch all afternoon?"

Calvin grinned, revealing brown teeth. "Just passin' time, Miss Grace."

"Well, pass it quieter," she said. "Or pass it somewhere else."

She turned back inside without waiting for a reply.

A moment later, the bell over the door jingled again.

Granville Smith Crockett stepped into the sunlight.

He was thin as a fence rail and stooped; the matted gray hair of his beard hung like Spanish moss from his chin. His dirty clothes were worn thin, with frayed sleeves and repatched boots. In one hand he carried a small sack of flour and a tin of lard. In the other, he held a gold coin, catching the light as he turned it over between his fingers.

Eli straightened.

The coin flashed once—bright as a wink—then disappeared into Grace's waiting palm as Granville paid. She gave him a nod and pushed the sack closer.

"You mind the heat now," she said.

He smiled faintly. "Heat don't bother me none."

"Course it don't," Calvin muttered. "Man don't sweat the same way the rest of us do."

Granville's gaze slid briefly to the brothers. It didn't linger. Didn't judge. It simply noticed.

Eli felt a flicker of recognition then, something old and unwelcome. His father had spoken the name Crockett once, years ago, in a voice meant to be private.

Then Granville turned and shuffled down the road toward the woods.

Calvin let out a low whistle. "Well, I'll be."

Thomas finally spoke. "That real?"

"Gold don't shine like that unless it is," Eli said.

They watched Granville until he vanished beyond the trees, where the dirt road narrowed and darkened.

"He ain't harvested a thing in years," Calvin said. "Ain't worked for nobody. Ain't sold nothin'. Yet he buys things with gold."

"Union gold," Eli said flatly, wiping his mouth with the back of his hand.

"I heard folks say it was Confederate gold. Bastard deserted and kept it for himself," Calvin added. "Stole it and ran. Left men dyin'."

Thomas shifted uneasily. His mouth opened as if to speak, then closed when Eli looked at him.

"They say he's buried it in jars. All over."

"Union didn't give a damn about men like us," Eli said. "Took what they wanted. If he ran away with their gold, he deserves what's comin'."

Eli's jaw tightened. "I seen men die," he said. "Bled out in the mud while officers talked about exemptions. Some men never made it to France at all." He eyed the crops, dying in the fields. "And I come home to this."

"Folks say a lot that ain't true," Calvin murmured. "But that coin was real enough."

Eli didn't answer right away. He stared at the place where Granville had gone, eyes narrowed, jaw working slowly.

"That old man don't need it," he said finally. "Not all of it."

Eli had seen how the world worked. Some men drank deep. Others licked the rim and called it living.

Grace's voice came sharp from inside the store.

"I'd mind what I say if I were you," she said. "You boys keep sayin' Crockett like it's one man. Out here, the ground doesn't always keep names straight."

Eli glanced toward the door, then spat again. "Ain't sayin' nothing wrong."

Grace stepped halfway out, shadowed by the doorway. "Some folks survive by keepin' to themselves. Some folks survive by mindin' their own business."

Calvin chuckled. "That old coot survived by taking care of himself at the expense of others."

Grace's eyes flicked to him. "That's usually enough to ruin a man."

She went back inside and closed the door.

The brothers stood in silence a moment longer, the cicadas rasping loudly in the trees.

"I didn't crawl through mud and blood just to come home and die poor," Eli said. "Not while men like him sit on what don't belong to them."

He stared at the road leading to Granville Smith Crockett's shack. "We'll meet after dark."

***

Night came thick and fast.

The lanterns bobbed as they moved, their yellow light carving narrow tunnels through the trees. The swamp breathed around them, wet, sour with the odor of decay, but alive. Mud sucked at their boots with every step, even with the drought.

The air was heavy, steamy, the kind that soaked through clothes and made skin slick.

Thomas shivered.

"You cold?" Calvin scoffed.

10

"I can see my breath," Thomas whispered. A thin white fog puffed from his mouth, despite the heat. "Air's changed. Somethin' ain't right."

Eli didn't slow. "You just keep up, now. You hear?"

They reached the shack near midnight. It leaned in on itself, as if the gentlest wind could blow it to bits. Its boards were dark and swollen, the roof sagging like the drought-ridden crops back on the farm. Behind it, firelight flickered—low and restless.

Granville stood in the clearing, a shovel in his hands.

Thirteen rusty Mason jars lay open at his feet, gold spilling from them like honey from a beehive. The fire cast the coins into a thousand glimmers, lighting his face from below.

For a moment, none of the brothers moved.

Then Calvin laughed.

Eli rushed him first.

The shovel dropped. Granville fell hard, his breath leaving him in a thin cry. Fists came down. Boots followed. The gold rang softly as the jars were kicked aside.

"Stop," Granville gasped, blood streaking his mouth. "You don't understand."

Eli grabbed him by the collar and dragged him upright. "We understand enough, old man."

Granville looked at the Gatlins—not pleading, not angry.

Only tired.

"Leave it," Granville said. "There's still time."

Thomas swallowed. "He said…"

Eli's look stopped him cold.

He shook his head once. "I've already paid for it."

Granville whispered. "I'm warnin' you."

"He's threatenin' us," Calvin snarled.

Calvin struck Granville again.

They hauled him to the water's edge and threw him in. The dark water of the swamp swallowed the old man without a splash. The surface closed over him, black and smooth.

11

Calvin laughed, then stopped.

They ran back to the shack, grabbing jars as their arms strained under the weight.

Then, the ground shifted.

Thomas screamed first.

The earth opened beneath them, sucking at their legs, boots, and knees. Their lanterns toppled, the light spinning wildly.

Eli cursed and thrashed. He understood how the world worked. He had never learned where its lines were drawn.

Calvin clawed at roots that broke in his hands.

The swamp pulled them down—not violently, not angrily, but with certainty.

And then they heard it.

Laughter.

Not from the water.

Not from the shack.

From everywhere.

Loud as thunder.

The ground swallowed their cries.

Silence followed, deep and absolute.

Then, slowly, the night resumed.

Crickets. Frogs. Wind in the reeds.

Behind the shack, the ground stayed wet.

And somewhere beneath it, something waited.

Nothing ever grew right in that ground again.

CHAPTER 3 — ILLUSION OF SECURITY

Labor Day 2025— Near Midnight
Culpeper County, Virginia

"I wonder what channels we can get on this thing?"

Ed Handley sat in the construction trailer's folding chair, his steel-toed work boots planted wide on the scratched linoleum floor. One hand reached into a bag of stale chips he had found on top of the refrigerator, while the other flipped through the channels, searching for the ball game.

The small television sat atop a metal filing cabinet in the corner, its flickering light dancing across the walls.

"The score is three to three." The announcer spoke in an easy tone, as if nothing were wrong in the world.

Outside, the jobsite lay quiet beneath a full moon. Thin clouds drifted across it, dimming the light just enough to soften the edges of the heavy equipment, which sat idle, caked with dust and damp soil. The temporary lights along the perimeter fence buzzed faintly, pushing back the dark into the scrub grass and cattails along a stream beyond the fence. Piles of dirt rose in low mounds beside shallow trenches cut for utility lines.

He leaned back in the chair, his hands clasped behind his head. This was the kind of job Ed liked. Easy money. Sit tight. Watch the fence. Call in if anything didn't belong.

"You're the fourth guard in a month," the supervisor had told him matter-of-factly during the orientation before the job. He said it like it was an "oh, by the way," the same tone used if there were a broken light or tools missing.

Ed had laughed at that. "People quit too easily on things these days," he told the supervisor, who hadn't laughed back.

No one had explained why the other guards wouldn't return, but when Ed tried to ask one of them, the man's face had gone pale so quickly it looked as if the blood had drained out all at once. He had shaken his head before Ed could finish the question.

"Confidential," the man had said. "I can't. Just be careful."

The extra pay made the shift worth it. That was what mattered. There was a baby on the way. Bills were piling up faster than they could be paid. Ed needed the money, and he wasn't the type to scare easily.

He adjusted the ballcap on his head, the security company's name stitched across the front in block letters, then leaned back in the chair. His dark blue uniform shirt clung to him, the white undershirt visible at the collar where he'd left the top button undone. Sweat had already worked its way down his back. A heat wave had settled over Northern Virginia nearly a week ago. Mid-90s by day, thick and steamy well past midnight. No breeze. No relief.

Ed wiped his fingers, greasy from the potato chips, on his pant leg and reached for the radio on the desk. It sat silent, its red indicator light steady.

The crack of the bat on television pulled his attention back. A fly ball arced into the outfield, heading toward the foul pole.

"Come on," Ed muttered.

Then a knock came on the trailer door.

Three sharp raps in succession. Not aggressive, but evenly spaced. Precise.

Ed muted the television. The sudden quiet inside the trailer made the sounds outside feel louder for a moment. Insects. A distant hum from the power lines. The faint buzz of the lights.

He glanced at the clock. 11:43.

Ed stood, took the flashlight from the hook by the door, and rested his hand on the handle. Another knock came, same rhythm.

He opened the door.

No one stood on the steps.

The light from the trailer spilled out onto the gravel. The ground beyond looked uneven and damp, darker than it should have been. Ed leaned out and scanned left, then right. No movement. No retreating footsteps.

"Yeah?" he called.

Nothing answered.

He stepped down onto the gravel, the flashlight beam sweeping low. The stones glistened faintly, darkened as if they'd been soaked hours ago—despite the forecast calling for continued dry weather. The sky was clear, and the moon was bright enough to make out a grader near the fence line.

"Who's there?"

Chirp. Chirp. Only crickets responded.

Shaking his head, Ed said more to himself than to the night, "Somebody messin' around."

A sharp snap sounded from the right.

A branch breaking. Close.

Ed turned slowly. The flashlight beam skimmed over stacked cinder blocks, a load of plywood, and the dark face of the trailer. Nothing moved.

He listened. The habit returned without effort, old and familiar.

Nothing.

Then another sound, softer this time, like something brushing through leaves.

Ed stepped away from the door and circled the trailer, the flashlight cutting through the shadows. The air felt thick and damp, carrying a smell that didn't belong on a several-month-old jobsite. Rot. Wet earth turned too deep.

When he rounded the last corner, the beam caught on letters smeared across the trailer's side.

GO.

The word was large and uneven, with heavy strokes. The material shone wetly in the light. Dark streaks ran downward, fresh trails that hadn't had time to dry yet.

Ed stared at it, irritation flaring first.

"What the hell is this?"

He had been inside. The door had been closed. Someone had done this while he sat just a few feet away.

The second thought came colder.

It looked like blood.

Not the bright red people expected. Darker. Thicker. Glossy in the light.

Ed had seen blood like that before. Not in stories. In real places where it smelled of copper and mingled with fear.

He stepped closer. The smell in the air sharpened.

"Cute," he said sarcastically.

He thumbed his radio. "This is Handley. Someone tagged the trailer. I'm checking the perimeter."

The radio crackled softly, then fell quiet.

Ed let out a short laugh and turned toward the tree line beyond the fence. The woods pressed close to the jobsite, dipping into low ground thick with brush. Beyond that lay older land, undisturbed for a long time, but soon to be cleared for a data center.

"Old property," the supervisor had said. "The shack's still back there. It looks like a good wind could blow it over. Don't go poking around."

A faint light appeared between the trees.

16

Not one of the perimeter lights. Not the moon. Something smaller, moving as if it were carried.

Ed narrowed his eyes.

"A lantern?" Muttering to himself, he asked, "What the hell is that doing out here?"

He stepped toward the fence. The ground gave slightly under his boots, spongy and damp.

"The site's closed," he called. "You need to head out."

No response.

The light drifted deeper into the trees.

Ed went through the gate, the chain-link fence rattling softly. The job-site lights faded almost at once, and the shadows thickened. The lantern's glow became the only point of warmth ahead.

The woods smelled wet and old. Mud squished underfoot, retaining moisture it shouldn't.

"Must be a stream here," he thought. "There's been no rain for ten days."

A gust of wind moved through the trees.

Cold. Sudden. It raised gooseflesh along Ed's arms and down his spine before vanishing.

He paused.

The night sounds carried on for a heartbeat longer. Insects. A distant owl.

Then they stopped.

Not fading. Not shifting.

Stopping.

Ed heard his own breathing, loud in the silence. The beam from the flashlight wavered, then steadied.

"Alright," he said quietly.

The lantern's light slowed.

17

Ed kept moving. Stopping would mean admitting that something was wrong.

The light halted completely. It hung between the trees, motionless.

Ed slowed. Shapes emerged in the moonlight. A fallen fence. A faint path. The outline of a low structure, hunched deeper in the woods.

The shack. Still standing.

Ed raised his flashlight, aiming it around the dangling light, searching for the hand that held it.

The beam caught nothing that made sense.

His eyes adjusted. The lantern's glow felt closer without moving.

His boot sank deeper into the wet ground. He pulled it free with a soft, sucking sound.

Ed swallowed and tried to speak.

There was no procedure for this.

What tore out of him instead was raw and absolute.

He screamed.

***

Monte Coleman pulled his truck through the jobsite entrance. Handley had checked in hours earlier. Because the message wasn't urgent, he had made his normal rounds.

"3 AM," he whispered, checking his watch. He stepped out of the truck and glanced around.

The trailer door swung back and forth, tapping against the metal siding. Tap. Tap.

"Ed?" There was no answer.

"Hey, Ed. It's Monte." Monte scanned the jobsite but saw nothing else out of the ordinary.

"Let's check it out." Monte declared, almost as a warning, as he entered the trailer.

Inside, the television screen had gone to static. The volume was low, but not muted, a soft hiss filling the room like someone breathing in the dark. Nothing was disturbed enough to explain Ed's absence.

Monte leaned against the desk, confusion crossing his face at first, then resignation.

He shook his head and pulled a pack of cigarettes from his pocket.

The cigarette dangled from his lips. As he went to light it, he stared past the trailer toward the trees and said quietly, "Lost another one."

The door kept swinging.

The night explained nothing.

CHAPTER 4 — THE SURVEYOR'S MISTAKE

Labor Day 2025 — 4:00 PM
Culpeper County, Virginia

It was 4:00 PM, and the intense humidity and ninety-degree heat of late summer still held Northern Virginia in a sweaty stranglehold. Even without a drop of rain for weeks, the jobsite's red clay remained a viscous ooze. It swelled under the wheels and treads of the heavy equipment and clung to boot heels. The long chorus of grasshoppers and crickets echoed from tall weeds, and the air behind the tree line shimmered, not from wind but from heat trapped low to the ground.

Two bulldozers idled near the marked square where a data center would be built. Orange tape hung from stakes marking the perimeter. The creek lay roughly a hundred yards downhill, surrounded by alder and scrub pine. You couldn't see the water, only the yellowing leaves of the willow trees whose wet feet reached for moisture. Despite the drought, the water level remained high enough for an occasional ripple to stir the surface.

The water was necessary. The data center's servers required constant cooling, and the stream nearby would provide it. Surprisingly, few in the community had objected to this plan.

A survey drone murmured softly as it rose, then leveled off at thirty feet and drifted toward the hollow. The operator, wearing a white hard hat, squinted in the sun, watching its path. Suddenly, the drone tilted, steadied, and then veered off course. It disappeared behind a screen of river birch.

"What the fuck?" The operator grumbled and manipulated the console, trying to regain control. He stared at his monitor, and a second later, the screen filled with gray.

BAM!

The drone struck something and fell to the ground with a thud. The hum was gone. The console beeped several times, signaling a malfunction. Then nothing.

"Again?" the foreman thundered. Jake Krantz was a broad man, deeply tanned along the V of his shirt and across his arms from months of working under the summer sun.

"I told you to keep it over the flagged line!" he angrily berated the drone operator.

"It was over the line," he countered, checking the controls once more.

"Do you know how much those damn things cost?" Krantz muttered.

"Something pushed it, boss."

"The wind?"

"There is no wind," the operator answered, scanning the tree tops.

Tempers were flaring, the heat resting on them like an old dog refusing to move.

Just then, a silver Ford Focus entered through the gate and parked at the edge of the access lane. Sunlight reflected off the hood and the crushed-granite gravel until the world felt like a single solid color. A woman in her late twenties stepped out, shading her eyes with one hand and her long blonde hair pulled back in a ponytail.

Putting on her Wayfarers, she looked across what had been her grandfather's lower pasture. Kudzu had overgrown the split-rail fence rows years earlier. Blackberry brambles had taken over the ditches. The pasture dipped and then fell away toward the creek. On topographical maps, the contour lines drew close together there, tight as thread.

Krantz saw her and waved half-heartedly. "You Harlan?"

"Yes," she answered. "Clara Harlan."

"You own this?"

"It owns me for now," she said, as if that would help.

He spat into the dust and nodded toward the staked square.

"We had good numbers until we got close to the hollow. Then the gears heat up, and the batteries drain as if you pulled the plug."

Jake started toward Clara, dragging his boot out of the viscous red clay.

"The soil should be cracked, but it keeps reading saturated, and we haven't had real rain in three weeks. I've got my boss on me about deliverables."

"Corporate already flagged this site once," Krantz added. "They don't want delays—just answers."

"And now Monte's telling me another night guard packed it in," Krantz added. "Said the guy got rattled and quit. Same story as the last one."

Krantz went on, "People are jumpy. I get it. The heat does that."

He stood next to Clara, shaking his head in frustration.

"You see my problems?" he said. "Schedules don't care about stories."

Clara felt a bead of sweat trickle down her back.

The heat felt like a blast furnace and smelled of iron. She sniffed the air and detected a faint dampness, which, given the recent dry weather, didn't belong. She couldn't place it, but something smelled older.

"I appreciate you coming out at all," she said. "I wanted to see it with you here. My attorney says the sale contract is solid if the environmental impact study is clean."

Krantz let out a short laugh and said sarcastically, "The County will love this. Last week, we sank a footing and hit a spring where there shouldn't be one. If this keeps up, they'll shut us down indefinitely."

The drone pilot trudged up, holding a cracked fuselage. Mud streaked the plastic, and a dried leaf clung to one rotor. He tilted the body so Clara could see the camera port, which was stained with a tea-colored film.

"That is inside the housing," he said. "I popped the seal, and it breathed on me."

"Breathed?" Krantz scoffed. "Machines do not breathe."

Biting his lip to keep his temper in check, the operator insisted, "I know what I felt."

Clara crouched to look. The film on the lens had a ripple, as if something had settled and then shifted. She was an IT Project Manager by trade; her mind was built on best practices and checklists. The part of her that balanced budgets ran through the problems.

Drones falling. Fogged lenses. Batteries failing in the heat. Trouble finding good help.

This was normal.

The other part of her—the one the old house in Culpeper had raised in long summer shadows—listened to the unseen creek and felt the skin at the back of her neck tighten, sudden and precise, as if something had taken notice.

"Let's try once more," she said. "Then we'll break for the day. I can show you the old foundation before you go. That will help you plot the utilities."

Krantz looked toward the trees. "Utilities," he said, and the word hung in the air for a moment, like a promise told to the wrong person.

They launched a second drone. It climbed in a steady arc and held its position over the marked line. The pilot breathed through his mouth and kept his hands still. The feed showed the field, the tape, the bulldozer tread marks, and the bright scar where a test pit had been dug and filled. The image vibrated in the heat. Then the horizon tilted. Not much. Just enough to make the eye notice it. The drone drifted toward the hollow as if a draft had carried it, though the map showed no wind. The trees below did not sway.

"Pull back, damn it!" Krantz shouted.

"I'm trying," the pilot said. His thumbs carefully guided the sticks.

The feed whitened. A gray wave rolled across the frame, then cleared. For a second, they saw the creek's dark ribbon and a patch of open water with a glassy sheen, like an oil slick. In the center, the water pulsed. A faint ring spread outward, bubbling at the edges.

The video cut to black. The drone fell through the canopy, a distant series of snaps sounding like tiny bones.

"Enough," Krantz said in disgust. "That is my last one."

He pulled off his hard hat and wiped the sweat from his face with his sleeve, then did not put it back on. The men shut down the bulldozers. The sudden silence was deafening.

A crew member lit a cigarette and took a single drag. He looked at the trees as if they had called his name. He ground the cigarette out under his boot and didn't take another drag.

"You mentioned an old foundation," Krantz told Clara. "Show me that so I can send a report. We'll call in a geotechnical engineer. If they find potential for swelling and high groundwater, the company will think twice."

Clara led them along the path that angled toward the creek. Grass hissed like a snake against their pant legs. The heat pressed down on their shoulders. A turkey vulture soared over them, then chose a different patch of sky.

The foundation lay beneath a thicket of sumac and honeysuckle, four lines of stones forming a rectangle, the outline of a house that had never been large enough to matter to anyone. A sycamore had pushed its roots under the western wall, lifting the corner by several inches. Charred material streaked one stone.

"Someone burned brush here," Clara said.

Glancing around, Krantz added, "or maybe more than just brush."

The smell rising from the hollow remained unchanged, but Clara noticed it for the first time. It wasn't rot, like in a swamp. It was the scent that wafts from wet clay when a shovel strikes it, turning the earth over to the light.

"My grandfather kept a shed on the land when I was a kid," she said. "He stored canning pots and old tools. After he got sick, no one came down here."

She did not mention that she had not been down here in years. The place held a silence that lingered like sweat in your hair. She also remembered that her grandfather had told her to stay in the upper field when, on a cloudless day, the ground smelled like rain.

Krantz knelt and pressed his hand into the soil between the stones. When he lifted it, his palm was wet. He rubbed his thumb across the moisture and watched the shine it left.

"How often does your creek flood?" he asked.

"It comes up in spring," Clara said. "It never gets this high."

"It seems like it already did," he said.

A light flickered beneath the sycamore roots. It could have been the sun, but the angle was wrong for that. Still, the mind always tries to protect you from yourself. The light shifted, revealing a small, round shape buried to its lip. Glass caught the sun and reflected it like a mirror.

Krantz spotted it, too. "What is that?"

"Junk," the pilot said quickly. He had stepped back from the stones and now kept both hands on his controller, as if the downed drone still needed steering.

Clara moved closer. Honeysuckle snagged on her jeans. She pushed last fall's leaves aside and felt the cool undergrowth against her wrists. The glass was old, thick at the rim, and bubbled within. A Mason jar, or what was left of one. It had no lid. The mouth was packed with silt the color of dried blood, and in the silt, something darker lay folded like a stain.

She didn't touch it. Not because she feared what was inside, though she did, nor because she feared a cut. She didn't touch it because the hair along her arms had lifted and stayed that way, and she could feel a slight breath on her skin, as if the ground had exhaled.

"We'll get a shovel," Krantz said, but he didn't move to grab it.

"Leave it," Clara said. The words surprised even her. "It's on my property. I'll catalog anything we find and call the county."

She looked at Krantz. "You can include that in your report. The owner requests that artifacts remain undisturbed."

Krantz studied her face for a moment. The insects filled the silence. Down in the trees, a woodpecker pecked at a dead trunk, and the sound echoed like an iron spike driven into a railroad tie.

"Fine," he said at last. "We'll pack up for the day and come back tomorrow with a larger crew and hopefully have a better day."

They emerged from the thicket into the late afternoon heat. The crew dismantled the launch table and gently placed the dead drone in a case, as if it were a fragile bird they didn't want to bruise. The generators coughed once, then went permanently silent. Trucks roared to life and lined up along the access road. A wayward gull from a nearby landfill to the east rode the thermal updraft and let out a cry.

Clara waited until the last diesel truck had gone. The silence that followed felt larger than the big orange ball that was the setting sun. It felt like a room after someone important had left, and the walls were deciding what to say about it.

She returned to the stones. The shade had shifted, casting a faint, merciful shadow over the rectangular foundation. She crouched by the sycamore and glanced at the glass again. A small bead of moisture had formed at the jar's mouth, something that hadn't been there before. It quivered, then slid back into the darkness of the container as if pulled by an invisible force.

"You don't get to be anything more than what you are," she told the ground. "You are dirt. You are water. You are mine, at least for now."

The answer, if there was one, came from farther away. It rose from the direction of the creek. It might have been a truck on Route 29. It could have been the wind. Or it might have been a man laughing under his breath, his cheek full of chewing tobacco.

Clara stood and brushed the clay from her hands. The marks it left on her jeans looked as if someone else had been touching her.

She stepped back out of the thicket and didn't turn her back on the foundation stones until she was in the open field again.

On her way to the car, she passed the flagged stakes. One had fallen over, and the tape lay on the clay, stuck there as if the ground had licked it and enjoyed the taste. She knelt to straighten the stake and paused. At the edge of the tape, half-sunk in the red soil, something clear and round winked. Not the jar she had seen—a different one. Smaller. Its rim showed a thin thread of rust where a lid had once been.

Clara did not dig. She set the stake upright, pressed the clay firmly around it with her palm, then headed to her car. When she closed the door, it felt cooler, as if the heat outside had been a person she had finally managed to shut out.

As she turned the key, the radio flicked on, tuning into a station she didn't recall selecting. Static crackled across the dial before settling into a sound like rain on a tin roof.

"...groundwater anomaly," the voice said. Then silence. Then a low chuckle that the radio struggled to tune in, like a laugh held underwater too long and now surfacing in bubbles—a sound that felt less like interference and more like timing.

Clara turned off the radio and kept both hands on the wheel until the trembling in her fingers eased. She drove beyond the line of stakes. The rearview mirror reflected the field as a tall, bright rectangle. For a moment, as the road climbed and the angle shifted, she saw the hollow soften. The clay seemed to settle, then swell again, like breath finally finding a rhythm.

The jar under the sycamore caught the light one last time and blinked. Then the leaves shifted, and it went back to sleep.

CHAPTER 5 — THE OLD MAN AT THE DINER

The next morning arrived heavy. Clouds hung low over Route 29 like smoke. Clara had stayed awake half the night, listening to the old farmhouse breathe. Every so often, a pop came from beneath the floorboards, soft yet wet. She convinced herself it was heat expansion, mice, or the humidity.

Still, she'd lain there waiting for the next sound, already knowing it would come.

By sunrise, she had packed her laptop and left the house.

The only restaurant open this side of Culpeper was the Last Stop Diner, a small white cinderblock building on a corner lot beside a feed store and an abandoned gas station advertising Ethanol-Free fuel. Clara parked in front. The asphalt shimmered in the heat as she exited the vehicle. The cicadas were already buzzing in the trees as she clicked the lock on the remote.

When she reached the door, the cicada chorus stopped.

A faded Coca-Cola sign out front read: *Air Conditioned Since 1962.* When Clara opened the door, a small brass bell jingled, and the smell of bacon grease and bottom-of-the-pot coffee wrapped around her like a familiar glove. The air inside was damp, like the scent after a thunderstorm.

She slid into a booth by the window. The vinyl seat hissed beneath her, sticky from the heat. She picked up a menu with yellowed edges, covered in plastic. The waitress was slim, with gray hair that shone like polished silver. She poured coffee without asking, into a cup with a chipped rim.

The coffee smelled faintly metallic beneath the bitterness.

Her badge caught Clara's eye as the woman set down the pot and pulled silverware wrapped in a paper napkin from her apron. Wydra Grace, it read, the letters faded from years of washing.

Clara glanced up. "That's an unusual name."

Wydra's mouth curved into a polite, practiced smile. "Old family name. From my mother's people. Folks around here shorten it to '*Wy*' if it makes 'em uncomfortable."

"It doesn't," Clara said.

"Good," Wydra replied lightly, picking up the coffee pot from the table.

"New face," she said. "Are you passing through or lost?"

"Maybe both," Clara said, managing a smile. "Inherited some land off Buck Run. Trying to figure out what to do with it."

The waitress paused mid-pour, her smile tightening. "You mean that old Harlan place?"

Clara nodded. "You know it?"

"Everyone does," Wydra Grace said quietly. "Though most wish they didn't. You're the Harlan girl, ain't you? Been away for a while. Your granddaddy came in here every Tuesday till he took sick."

Clara nodded. "Guess that makes me the Harlan woman now."

Unaffected by the sarcasm, Wydra asked, "That land still yours, darlin'?"

"For now," Clara answered with a sigh, staring out the window.

The waitress smirked as if ownership were an idea that didn't impress her, then went to refill another customer's cup.

As she passed, her hand brushed the edge of Clara's table, then stopped short, as if she'd already decided she wouldn't touch whatever belonged in that space.

Across from Clara, sitting at the counter, a man cleared his throat. He had been sitting there before she entered. She hadn't noticed him because he sat so still. His long-sleeved shirt was buttoned to the collar despite the heat. He wore a sweat-darkened cap and a khaki vest covered in Civil War reenactment patches. His stringy white hair fell to his shoulders, and he looked at her with dark eyes, the color of wet clay.

29

Clara nodded, and his eyes drifted until they settled on her. His gaze lingered, not suspicious, but recognizing. "You're a Harlan," he said.

She blinked. "Was, on my mother's side."

He got up and took a seat across from her without asking. His hands were large, their skin sun-cracked and patterned like old bark. He smelled faintly of pipe tobacco and sweat.

"Name's Ephraim Tate. I keep the records for the historical society... what's left of it. Folks used to call me the keeper of the dead."

He seemed to reconsider that, then added: "Or maybe just the one who remembers where they stay put."

He stirred a sugar packet into his coffee. "Guess that makes us kin, sort of."

For a moment, only the hum of the ceiling fan broke the silence. It clicked once, missed a beat, then resumed its slow rotation.

Clara laughed, uncertain whether he was joking. "And what exactly do the dead need keeping for?"

"They don't," he said. "It's for the living who forget 'em too easily."

Then Ephraim leaned forward.

"I heard they're planning to build a data center over there."

She sipped from her cup and then responded, "That's the plan if the sale passes inspection."

"Won't," he said flatly. "Buck Run won't have it."

Ephraim leaned back.

"You're stirring up ghosts, miss," he said.

Clara blinked. "Excuse me?"

He pointed toward the window, to the distant fields invisible behind the courthouse.

"Buck Run. Your family's land. I've seen the trucks out there."

She smiled politely. "Progress always stirs things up."

His chuckle was a dry sound, like wind through cornstalks.

"That piece of earth of yours doesn't take kindly to progress. The last man who tried to tame it ended up feeding it."

"Ridgely Smith Crockett," Clara said before she could stop herself. The name felt heavier in her mouth than she expected.

She asserted, "Everybody's got a version of that story."

"Names don't sit still out in the hollow," the old man said. "Folks say Crockett and mean whichever one haunts 'em."

He leaned in again. His breath faintly reeked of a mix of coffee and tooth decay.

"My great-granddaddy fought with Crockett's unit in the Wilderness. Til the day he died, he said Crockett deserted with a mule cart full of payroll gold. Took the money and left with the devil's blessing."

Ephraim slid his finger under his cap and scratched his head.

"There's a part of the story folks don't tell," he said, then stopped, jaw tightening.

"Folks say he buried Satan's blessing in them jars, so it'd guard what he stole."

Clara kept her eyes on the coffee. "Stories keep people entertained."

"Sometimes," Ephraim paused before saying it softly, "they keep people alive, too."

He wiped his chin and continued, "Your granddaddy knew that. He came to me once, several years ago, and asked if I could help find where the jars were hidden. Said he wanted to dig 'em up and burn whatever came out. But he lost his nerve. Told me later the land didn't want strangers diggin'."

Ephraim's hand trembled slightly as he lifted his cup. "He died the next season. That was the last good spring water Buck Run ever gave."

Outside, thunder rolled across the Piedmont hills.

The waitress looked up.

"The forecast said clear," she muttered.

31

Ephraim smiled dryly. "That hollow doesn't take orders from forecasts."

Clara forced out a laugh. "You sound like one of my granddad's sermons."

"I sound like somebody who's seen a man drown on dry ground," Ephraim said.

Clara raised an eyebrow, saying, "So, the creek has voting rights now?"

He didn't smile. "That land remembers what was done to it. Remembers who's buried beneath it, too. It's a place of debts."

"What kind of debts?"

He tapped his fingers on the table. "Ever hear the real story of Ridgely Smith Crockett?"

She shook her head.

Old Confederate quartermaster. Deserted the army near Brandy Station, took his regiment's pay in gold coins, and buried 'em along the Rappahannock. Ended up in those woods near your place, half-mad and whispering to the ground. Folks said he could hear the river talk.

Clara sipped her coffee. "That's a good ghost story."

"'Cept it ain't just a story," he said. "Crockett died in those woods — beaten by three men with your last name."

The words hit her harder than she expected. For a moment, she remembered being a child, standing barefoot at the edge of the creek, feeling the mud pull at her heels as if it didn't want to let go.

"You're saying—"

"I'm saying the Harlans took his gold, dumped his body in Buck Run, and never saw another sunrise between 'em. Storm came that night and washed their tracks away. The bodies were never found. After that, every Harlan who tried to make something of that land met with bad luck. You think your company will be any different?"

Clara frowned, torn between disbelief and a lingering sense of unease she couldn't shake.

"You actually believe that?"

Ephraim's gaze drifted to the window, where the clouds sagged like bruises. "Belief ain't the word. The earth holds memory. Crockett was greedy, but he died guarding what he loved. Your kin died taking what wasn't theirs. And the land... well, the land never forgot which side it was on."

He slid a folded paper napkin across the table.

"Listen, Miss Harlan. You're blood to those who wronged Crockett. If you go diggin', you'll find more than metal and mud. That creek keeps what it's owed."

Clara glanced down, and on the napkin was a crude hand-drawn map: the outline of the Harlan property, the curve of the creek, and a small X under a scribbled word:

Cellar

"I don't need..." Clara started, but he was already on his feet. His old knees cracked like gunfire.

"Keep it. You'll remember where not to dig."

Then he reached into the pocket of his vest and handed her a photocopy of an old ledger page — yellowed, with faded ink. At the top, it read *Survey of Crockett Holdings, 1871*. A rough map sketched the area: the creek, the hill, and a small mark labeled *13 jars*.

Clara felt the hair stand up on her arms. "Where did you get this?"

"Culpeper Archives," he said. "Found it after the flood in '93. It matches the spot where your pasture stays wet. You see this part here?" He pointed to a symbol beside the creek — a circle with a line through it. "Old conjure mark. A binding spell. Crockett wasn't just hiding gold. He was keeping something in."

Clara folded the paper and slipped it into her bag. "I'll take a look."

Ephraim's eyes sharpened. "Don't. Leave it be. That ground ain't yours to wake."

For a fleeting, stubborn moment, Clara resented the certainty in his voice about something that had never asked her permission.

He dropped a few bills on the table, nodded at the waitress, and slowly limped back to the counter, as if he had all the time in the world and had seen what came after it.

Clara had lost her appetite and left the diner before he could say another word. The bell above the door jingled once, then fell quiet. Outside, the sky had taken on a tin-like hue. Somewhere to the west, thunder rumbled.

Clara looked back through the window. Ephraim still sat there, motionless, one finger tracing the edge of his coffee cup as if drawing circles in the dirt.

She realized then he hadn't warned her where to dig—only where not to.

He wasn't just an old man at a diner. He was someone who knew the shape of the ground when it opened.

She unfolded the napkin again. The ink had smudged slightly from his damp fingers. Beneath the word 'cellar,' he had written something else in shaky block letters:

DON'T LISTEN IF IT LAUGHS.

When she reached her car, she noticed something on the windshield — a single coin, damp despite the dry air. It was old, dulled to a green patina, with a worn emblem she didn't recognize. She turned it over and saw faint letters pressed into the metal:

R.S.C.

She dropped it as if it were burning.

The coin hit the pavement, rolled toward the storm drain — and then stopped.

Just before it hit the grate, it tipped over once, then twice, and settled upright, balancing perfectly on its rim.

Its edge faced Buck Run.

CHAPTER 6 — THE JAR BENEATH THE FLOOR

The house was smaller than Clara remembered.
She had grown up visiting it on weekends, her grandfather's place beyond the railroad tracks and power lines, where the woods pressed close, and frogs croaked loudly. Now the frogs were gone. The air outside was dry and still. The smell drifting through the floorboards reminded her of the jar from the jobsite — the same wet, iron-like sweetness, like freshly turned earth.

She paused on the threshold, uneasy without knowing why, then went in anyway.

She pushed the door in; it stuck briefly in the jamb before she turned on the light. The bulb flickered before coming to life, casting a pale reflection across the kitchen. The pastel yellow wallpaper, with its pattern of blood-red cherries, had peeled in long curls. On the counter sat a glass jar with cloudy residue clinging to the glass, filled with dead daisy stems, their petals scattered across the linoleum floor.

"Pappy loved daisies."

Clara knew the flowers were her grandfather's doing — the last thing he must have placed there.

She moved slowly through the rooms, making a mental list of what needed to be cleared before the sale. Each step stirred up dust that hung in the air.

The sound began in the back hallway.
A slow, deliberate drip echoed through the floorboards. She crouched and pressed her ear to the wood. The air beneath her was damp and cool — cooler than the rest of the house.

"Can't be a leak," she muttered.

She found the old trapdoor in the pantry, the one her grandfather used to store preserves in the crawl space. The latch protested as she pulled it open. The smell that rose made her empty stomach turn — soil, mold, and a faintly sweet scent, like fruit long gone to rot.

35

Clara shone her phone's light down the wooden ladder. The beam cut through dust and spiderwebs, catching the glint of glass below.

"Of course," she said. "More jars."

She climbed down. The dirt floor was damp enough to squish under her boots. Jars were everywhere — some upright, some toppled, all coated in mud. Dozens. The light highlighted faint letters scratched into a few lids: H, L, and a crooked C.

"Pappy," she whispered. "What the hell were you doing down here?"

One jar sat apart from the others, directly beneath a floor joist. Its lid was rusted shut. Something inside flickered where she shone her light — not gold exactly, more like oil reflecting it.

She reached out. Her fingers brushed the lid, and the jar shifted. Just a tremor, as if something had stirred.

Clara froze.

The air grew thick, a hush settling over the space. Then a faint trickle sounded. She directed her light toward the sound. Water was seeping in from the seam where the foundation met the ground — black and slow, winding through the dirt toward her boots.

She stepped back, her heartbeat loud in her ears.

"Just groundwater," she said aloud.

But the words didn't steady her. The dripping had changed. It was no longer random — it had a rhythm. Like a pulse. Like something counting.

Drip.

Pause.

Drip.

Pause. Then— a breath.

It seemed to come from the jar. She sensed it before she heard it: a whisper of air brushing her face, cool and damp; an exhaled sigh that had waited a century to escape.

She grabbed the jar and climbed the ladder, her heart pounding. The rungs shook under her boots. She didn't stop until she was back in the pantry, holding the jar tight to her chest, as if it might bite her if she let go. The trapdoor slammed shut behind her, sealing the darkness below.

When she looked down, moisture had pooled at the base of the jar, darkening the floorboards.
She leaned in closer. The glass had fogged from the inside.
A shape — faint, cloudy, human — briefly pressed against the inner wall, as if testing it. Then it vanished.

The floor beneath her creaked.
And from deep below in the earth, something laughed — not loud, not echoing, but soft and close, as if it were right beneath her feet.

CHAPTER 7 — THE MAN IN THE MUD

The summer of 1871 lingered like a fever. Cicadas screamed in the pines, and the leaves of the hardwoods moved not a bit; green statues, a living testament to the heat and humidity. The Rappahannock River, on its way to the Chesapeake Bay, crept through the Piedmont, thick and sluggish, its surface coated with green scum. On its banks, Ridgely Smith Crockett labored with his shovel through soil that bled red as he turned it.

He'd come back from the war, thin as a stick and twice as tough. Some said he'd deserted before Appomattox; others whispered he'd killed his commanding officer for the pay chest. Whatever the truth, he built his shack on the edge of Buck Run Creek, a one-room hut of cedar planks with a tarpaper roof, and set about making himself invisible.

By day, he trapped muskrats and skinned them for pennies. By night, he kept digging. Always digging. He remembered what his brother Granville said, "There were two types of men in the world. Those who dig and those who die."

Neighbors saw his lantern moving among the trees after midnight. They'd hear the scrape of metal and the low sound of his voice—sometimes talking to himself, other times to something that answered back.

He stored the gold in mason jars he scavenged from the ruins of a burned-out farmhouse. Thirteen jars in all. He wondered sometimes about the number thirteen. He had once been told that thirteen was a number only special people could handle. He didn't know if he felt special or burdened.

He washed each jar with creek water, polished the lids with lard, and lined them along the shack's wall. Why? The hell if he knew.

When the moon was high, he'd dig them up, pour the coins onto the dirt floor, and run his fingers through them until his skin split.

He convinced himself it wasn't greed, just insurance. He'd seen what the world did to men who trusted it.

Then, the land began to change around him. The ground stayed wet even during the drought. Trees near the shack grew thin and pale, and sometimes, when he knelt in the mud to bury a jar, the earth seemed to shift beneath him—just slightly, enough that his shovel felt lighter, as if the ground had opened to accept an offering.

***

One night, the moon rose red and low. The air smelled of lightning, as if a storm were rolling in, even though the sky was clear. Crockett lit his lantern and stepped barefoot into the yard, his spade slung over his shoulder.

He paused at the spot where he'd buried the first jar years earlier. The soil there pulsed faintly, moist with bubbles rising to the surface. He knelt, placed his hand on it, and whispered the verse he'd composed for himself.

Earth to clay, clay to gold.
What I keep will never grow old.

The ground responded with a soft pop, the sound of suction releasing. Mud bubbled. Something gold flickered beneath the surface. Crockett smiled and dug faster.

His shovel struck glass, then he lifted the jar free. Inside, the coins glowed faintly in the lantern light, but beneath them—he swore—something else moved. A ripple, a blink, like an eye opening.

Ridgely Smith Crockett dropped the shovel and crouched closer. He tipped the jar, watching the coins slide and settle, telling himself it was trapped water shifting in the heat.

The water inside the jar trembled; a faint voice hissed through the seal, dry and curious.

You keep what belongs to me, Ridgely Smith Crockett.

He froze. His lips split into a grin that looked more like pain than joy. "Ain't yours," he said. "I earned it."

Then bleed.

A sting pricked his palm. Blood trickled down his wrist, thick and dark, splattering onto the lid. The jar absorbed it. The mud shifted beneath his feet.

Ridgely Smith Crockett laughed—a wet, low sound. He pressed his thumb against the cut, smearing blood across the glass, then whispered, "Now it's paid for—for now."

Lightning flashed without thunder. In its white burst, the wind bent the trees backward, their leaves turned inside out. When the light faded, the creek was at his knees, warm and moving against him, circling, testing, though it hadn't rained.

***

In the following weeks, no one saw Ridgely Smith Crockett in town.

Children who dared to cross his property reported jars half-buried in the bank, their lids turning as if something inside wanted out. Dogs refused to drink from the creek. When hunters passed near the hollow, they found the ground soft underfoot, as if someone had tilled it from below.

By autumn, his lantern no longer moved through the trees. Only the laugh remained—thin, broken, carried on the fog that rolled in from Buck Run before dawn.

When the first frost arrived, the river froze overnight, trapping the reeds and driftwood. In the morning sun, the ice shimmered red, and beneath it, something sparkled like metal—a circle of jars resting in the silt. Their lids tight… waiting.

CHAPTER 8 — THE BROTHERS' PACT

Clara sat on the front steps, turning the mason jar slowly in her hands. The glass was warm from the sun, faintly tacky with residue she couldn't identify. She wiped her palm against her jeans.

As a child, her grandfather had used the pantry to preserve fruit and vegetables. Now she had no idea what he'd been doing down there. She gathered her hair and tied it in a ponytail. A late-afternoon breeze rustled the leaves and cooled the sweat on her neck.

The woods encircled the house, and she eyed them warily. She'd played there as a child, always with caution. She saw the fire pit and remembered roasting marshmallows with her grandfather. He loved to talk about local legends, and she recalled one in particular. To her, it was more than a story. It was a warning.

Her grandfather's voice rose in her mind, steady and low, …the way it always sounded when he was telling the truth.

The summer of '58 was exceptionally dry. No rain fell for six weeks. Only red dust and the scent of hot asphalt filled the air. Corn withered in the fields. Water levels in the wells dropped an inch each morning.

And down in Buckland Hollow, where Buck Run flowed through clay and ironweed, the Harlan brothers were plotting to steal a dead man's gold.

They lived in an abandoned sawmill, three miles from town. Earl, the oldest at thirty, was barrel-shouldered, with a mean streak carved into his smirk. Dean, two years younger, had eyes that never stopped moving, quick and nervous as a fox. The youngest, Tommy, barely twenty, tried to pretend his brothers' talk about Ridgely Smith Crockett was just the whiskey talking.

That night, the three of them sat on milk crates around a campfire built from railroad ties, passing a mason jar of corn liquor back and forth. A radio inside the shack picked up more static than music.

Earl spat into the dirt. "You know what's under that swamp? Forty pounds of Confederate gold. My buddy Skeeter from the quarry says it's marked on an old survey map. It belonged to a crazy bastard named Ridgely Smith Crockett."

Dean snorted. *"Old ghost story. Folks say Crockett's still out there, laughing when the moon's high."*

"Ghosts don't buy groceries," Earl said. *"And we're fresh out."* He poked the fire, sending sparks into the dark. *"Crockett buried that money in jars. Thirteen of 'em. He never had kin. Never spent a dime."*

Tommy nervously tugged at the label on his beer. *"We start diggin', people'll see. The sheriff'll be on us."*

Earl's smile widened. *"Sheriff? He don't come down that way. No one goes near that creek after dark. They're all afraid. Say the creek smells wrong. Too many stories."*

Dean leaned forward, eyes glittering. *"What kinda stories?"*

Earl's voice dropped to a whisper. *"They say that when Crockett died, the swamp took him back. Swallowed him whole. When the moon is full, you hear a voice comin' up from the mud. Like he's countin' what's his."*

The wind moved through the trees. Suddenly chilled, Tommy rubbed his arms. *"Maybe we oughta' wait till morning."*

Earl stood, tossing the empty jar into the fire, where it flared as the glass shattered. *"You wait, you starve. You move, you eat. Tonight, the moon's right."*

He slung a shovel over his shoulder and handed another to Dean. He tossed the third to Tommy, who caught it with reluctance. *"You're comin'. You're blood. That means you dig."*

***

Despite the heat, Clara shivered as a gust of wind rushed over her. She hadn't realized how late it had gotten and found it was nearly dark. As she headed toward the truck, she heard her grandfather's voice again.

The Harlans followed an old logging road toward Buck Run, Earl's pickup truck headlights cutting through the dust. Crickets chirped loudly in the ditches. When they reached the creek, fog drifted low over the water, thick as smoke.

The ruins of Ridgely Smith Crockett's shack still stood—four walls slumped inward, the roof gone, and a chimney leaning like a drunken man against a wall. The smell hit first: wet earth, then a metallic tang beneath, a scent that burned the back of your throat.

Dean muttered, "Feels like walkin' into a blacksmith's forge."

Earl jabbed him with the shovel handle. "Shut up and start diggin'."

They chose a spot near the chimney where the ground sloped downward. The first shovelful revealed dark, wet soil, black as tar, unlike anything they'd ever seen. By the time they dug knee-deep, the pit began to fill with seeping water that glistened like oil.

"Ah, hell," Earl said. "We're in the floodplain."

Then Dean's shovel struck glass with a dull clink. He knelt, trembling as he brushed away mud with shaky fingers. "Got somethin'."

He pulled up a mason jar, its thick glass now smoky with age. Inside, coins gleamed in the lantern light.

Gold coins.

Earl opened the jar, ran his fingers through the mud inside, and laughed, a deep, hungry sound. "Told you. Thirteen of 'em are somewhere in here."

They dug faster, mud flying and hearts pounding. They pulled up another jar, then another. Each was heavier than the last, with coins inside warm to the touch.

Tommy stood apart, watching the fog roll off the creek. It moved strangely — not drifting but crawling closer inch by inch, as if something beneath the surface were pushing it. "Earl," he said, "we got enough. Let's go."

Earl didn't respond. He crouched over the fourth jar, trying to loosen the lid. "Just one look," he said.

The seal broke with a hiss, like breath slipping from lungs.

The air shifted. The insects fell silent. Even the creek fell quiet.

From the hole in the ground, a sound emerged — a low, bubbling, wet noise. Then came laughter. Faint at first, then louder, closer behind them.

Dean swung the lantern toward the shack. In the doorway stood a figure: tall, thin, covered head to toe in slick black mud.

Eyes like candle flames through fog.

Ridgely Smith Crockett.

Earl stepped back, clutching the jar. "What the hell—"

The figure stepped forward, each movement a slurp of water and suction. Its mouth opened, and the voice that emerged was layered and gurgling as water, bugs, and mud spilled out.

"You got that right. You boys came to dig. There's room for three more."

Dean yelled. Tommy dropped his shovel and sprinted toward the truck. Earl threw the jar, and it shattered against Crockett's chest. The coins hit the ground and sank immediately, swallowed by the earth.

The laughter grew louder, echoing all around them. The ground trembled. Earl turned to run—but the earth gave way beneath him. He sank waist-deep in seconds, clawing at the edge of the hole as the mud rose. Dean reached to grab him, but the pull dragged them both down, down until only their hands were visible. Then those too disappeared.

Tommy made it halfway to the truck before the fog thickened around him. The headlights flickered. The fog closed in on Tommy. He slipped, went down hard, and the mud closed over his boots like hands. As he struggled, he heard it—quiet now, almost gentle—counting.

One.

The creek rose to his chest.

Two.

The last thing Tommy Harlan felt was the ground pulling him home.

The next morning, the hollow was quiet. The creek flowed as it always had. But the ground near the chimney stayed wet, no matter how hard the sun beat down.

And if a man stood there long enough, he could still hear it — a cackle rising from beneath the clay, patient and pleased, counting to thirteen.

Clara shuddered. Ephraim's story about the Harlan brothers and Ridgely Smith Crockett's gold took hold of her thoughts. Had history repeated itself? Clara tightened her grip on the jar until the glass bit into her palm. Ephraim hadn't told the story to scare her. He'd told it to prepare her.

Whatever her grandfather had tried to bury in the cellar hadn't stayed buried.

And the land, she realized now, never forgot its debts.

CHAPTER 9 — THE CURSE AND THE SILENCE

The truck hadn't started.

She'd tried twice, then a third time, listening to the engine turn and die—the sound carrying across the yard and vanishing into the trees. No lights came on in the house. No neighbors stirred.

She told herself she'd only go back inside long enough to wait it out.

Clara didn't know why she'd come looking for the folder—only that her hands were already on the drawer. She wasn't sure why, but she knew what would be in the folder she'd found years earlier in the bottom drawer of her father's old desk—and why she'd never opened it. Under the blotter, she found the C.H. she'd carved as a child and traced the letters with her finger.

The desk was a family heirloom, and with it came a part of the story her grandfather had kept hidden. Clara opened the folder and found pages torn from a diary or journal—different hands, different years, stitched together by years of silence. She began to read:

Morning broke bright over Buck Run the day after the storm, but no one in town wanted to go near it. The Harlan boys were gone. Folks already knew the hollow would keep its secrets.

Sheriff Daniels sent Deputy Burkett and two farmhands out anyway. They came back pale and shaking.

"The ground ain't right," one of them said. "Soft where it shouldn't be, and the air tastes like pennies."

They discovered tattered clothing a week later, caught in a tangle of willow roots two miles downstream. In the shirt pocket was a matchbook from the Last Stop Diner. Nothing else was found. No bones. No bodies.

Earl's truck sat abandoned on the logging road, its windshield cracked from top to bottom. The keys still hung in the ignition. The metal had rusted overnight.

After that, the town stopped asking questions.

***

They always did when it came to Buck Run. Only stories remained. If she asked questions, she got only more stories. Clara glanced out the window. It was pitch black outside. All she heard in the room was the grandfather clock's pendulum. She exhaled deeply and read on.

The sheriff dismissed it as an accident—"probable drowning due to flood conditions"—but the report was lost when the county offices flooded.

The paper was gone, but the talk never faded.

For years afterward, hunters claimed to hear laughter rising from the creek at dusk... jars lodged in the silt, their lids rusted shut. A few brave souls opened them. They said the air that came out smelled of blood and rain, and sometimes—just sometimes—they thought they heard voices whispering from the water.

The Harlan name lost its standing. The brothers' mother nearly went insane before winter ended. She claimed she saw her boys in the fog some nights, waist-deep in the creek, reaching for her. She died a year later on the banks of Buck Run, clutching a handful of wet clay.

By the mid-60s, the rest of the family had moved north to Bristow, where no one knew what their name meant. The land stayed in the family's records, though no one returned to claim it. When the taxes went unpaid, and the county marked it as abandoned due to unstable ground, it passed quietly to the Harlans. No questions asked.

When the interstate was built in the '70s, heavy equipment carved a straight scar through the foothills.
They said the ground near Buck Run swallowed excavators.
The project was rerouted without explanation.
The foreman quit, packed up, and moved to Florida the following week.

After that, nature reclaimed it — blackberry thickets, cottonwood, and kudzu creeping over the last stones of Ridgely Smith Crockett's foundation. The locals forgot, or at least pretended to. But the water remembered. It never ran clear. Every spring flood carried red silt downstream, staining the shallows like blood.

***

Back in the present, a storm was forming over the Blue Ridge. The heat that had intensified all day, pressing down on Culpeper like a thumb on a bruise, finally brought the heavens to life.

CLAP!

The thunder jolted a dazed Clara, who had scribbled notes on a sheet of paper:

Tommy Harlan had a son, Harold.

Harold had a son, Leon.

Leon had a daughter.

Clara.

"Jesus," she muttered. "Tommy Harlan was Grandpa's father…"

She let the realization sink in.

She wondered whether her grandfather, the boy raised in their family home in Bristow, grew up without knowing this.

Her Grandpa told stories about the Harlan boys, but the only thing she knew was that, when she asked, her father said the family records had been lost. Tommy Harlan's name was never spoken.

"He had to know," Clara whispered. "That's why he bought the old farmhouse with its gray clapboards, dated furnishings, and pantry filled with mason jars. It's why he walked the edge of Buck Run instead of crossing it, and why he watched."

The smell that clung to the mud on his boots when he returned was moldy, heavy. She never forgot it.

"I remember challenging each other to spend a night there." She chuckled, thinking of playing truth or dare with her friends. The smile quickly faded from her face. "None of them ever made it until dawn."

Clara's eyebrows drew closer as she tried to put the pieces of the puzzle together. "Was he keeping watch?"

Upon Grandpa's passing, his will left the property to Clara's father.

Leon.

He had died in a psychiatric hospital when she was a child. After that, she spent the summers with Grandpa until she went away to college. Mom never talked about the land, and she didn't remember much about her father, except that he sometimes woke up screaming in the night.

Clara would go to see what was wrong.

Biting her fingernails, she recalled his hands clawing at the sheets. As if the mattress were pulling him under. Her mother would tell her to go back to bed, but between gasps, her father would whisper.

"What was it?" She pressed her fingertips to her temples, trying to remember.

She closed her eyes and clenched her fists. Then it spilled out of her.

Let it be.

Don't dig.

***

At the edge of Buck Run, beneath the same sycamore that had witnessed every death and every lie, the ground shifted. Bubbles rose in a puddle that hadn't been there that morning.

One popped, releasing a soft hiss of air — like a man exhaling after holding his breath too long.

And underneath, faint yet definite, came a laugh that belonged to no one alive—answered, at last, by someone who remembered.

CHAPTER 10 — THE THIRTEEN JARS

The rain started abruptly. No wind, no thunder, only a single drop on the porch rail, then another. When Clara reached the window, the sky was a blanket of gray, like ash after a fire. The storm hit the siding like a freight train, and the noise of raindrops drowned out everything else: the buzz of the transmission lines, the hum of the refrigerator, and the faint whisper of the house.

She stood, watching the rain bruise the dirt. It didn't bead or run off. It soaked in, swallowed by the ground, which had been thirsty for months. The soil drank it faster than the rain could fall.

When the thunder finally arrived, it boomed like the artillery range at the Marine Base at Quantico, sometimes heard as far away as her childhood home in Bristow.

She tried to return to work, sitting at the kitchen table with her laptop open and the county estate tax forms half-filled out. But the Wi-Fi kept disconnecting, and every time she looked toward the window, the trees seemed closer than before.

***

By late afternoon, the power went out for good. The silence that followed was smothering. Even the rain held its breath, waiting for something to happen.

Clara took a flashlight from the emergency kit under the sink and carried it into the hallway. Fortunately, the batteries were still good, and the beam cast long, flickering shadows on the walls. As she passed the crawl-space door, she felt the draft — damp, cold, and slow, crawling across the floor. The same smell returned: wet iron, earth, and a faint, sweet scent beneath, like rotting fruit.

She knelt, reached for the latch, then pulled her hand back before finally summoning the courage to touch it.

The metal was warm beneath her fingers, as if it had been handled only moments before.

She knew it was wrong. She lifted the door anyway.

The ladder glistened with condensation. Somewhere below, water dripped steadily — slow, measured.

She called out, "Who's down there?"

No answer, only the sound of air moving, like an exhale, as if the house were sighing through its beams and rafters.

She knew she should close the door.

Instead, she grabbed her flashlight and went down.

***

The crawl space was shin-deep in mud, and the beam from her flashlight reflected off the moist sheen… and off something else. Dozens of glass jars had surfaced from the floor, their lids corroded and metal edges gleaming like teeth. They formed a pattern — a widening circle centered on the spot where she'd found the first one.

She counted aloud. "One, two, three…"

By the time she uttered thirteen, the air seemed heavy enough to feel.

"Humidity," Clara muttered.

Her breathing grew shallow. The flashlight flickered.

"Not now," she shook the light. "Don't go out now."

The beam returned, shining in the center of the circle. There sat the jar she'd uncovered on the jobsite days earlier — the one she'd found under the sycamore. It pulsed softly, as if lit from within.

"Phosphorescence," she told herself. "Old minerals sometimes did that."

She moved closer. Mud clung to her boots. "This isn't real," she whispered. "It's just old groundwater seeping up."

The jar's lid turned slowly, the metal groaning against rust. Whatever had been sealed there had not been sleeping. It had been waiting.

She froze.

Then — a single click, as if a latch had released.

The lid came off.

A gust of cold, damp air swept out. It carried the smell of river water and blood. Somewhere above her, the memory of the kitchen lights flickered orange, then dimmed. For a moment, she thought she saw shapes moving inside the glass—faces, faint as smoke, with wide, watchful eyes.

One of the other jars cracked, sharp as gunfire. Then another. And another.

The mud at her feet began to move — not sink, not slide, but breathe. Each breath bubbled up through the clay like a low, wet laugh.

Something brushed her ankle — slick and warm.

She stumbled backward, slipped, and hit the ground hard. The flashlight spun away, but its beam illuminated the jars simultaneously — thirteen circles of dim light staring back.

The laugh came again, clearer now, deep and layered. It filled the space like water in a well.

Thirteen for sin.
Thirteen for blood.
Thirteen jars to keep the flood.

Clara grabbed the flashlight, scrambled to her feet, and hurried up the ladder, her boots slipping. She slammed the trapdoor shut and leaned against it, gulping for air. Her hands trembled so much that she dropped the flashlight.

Through the wood beneath her, she felt the pulse persist — slow, steady, and alive.

Every few seconds, another thud came, like a heart trying to recall its rhythm.

***

When dawn arrived, the storm was gone. The air smelled fresh. She stepped onto the porch, blinking at the sunlight, and stopped cold.

The field in front of the house was covered in thirteen evenly spaced rings of dark, wet soil. The field had lain fallow and unmarked the day before. At the center of each ring, a jar half-buried, lids faintly gleaming in the morning sun.

And from the farthest ring — nearest the creek — came a thin, rippling sound.

It was laughter.

CHAPTER 11 — VOICES BENEATH THE RAIN

The storm had broken, but it didn't pass. It settled into the soil, the air, and her skin. The world outside the farmhouse was heavy and bright, every blade of grass shimmering like glass beads. Buck Run had risen, a sluggish brown vein creeping over its banks, shutting the jobsite down until the water receded.

The thirteen rings on the field remained.

Clara stood at the window in her grandfather's favorite shirt, a mug of coffee cooling in her hands. She'd found tea-light candles in a drawer and heated enough water for Sanka. She needed it after last night.

She hadn't slept since the jars had started cracking. She told herself she'd go out and bury them again, seal them away, call the county inspector, call anyone. But every time she tried to step off the porch, the air grew thick, humid, humming, faintly electric, as if the ground were listening for her footsteps.

It wasn't fear that held her back. It was the feeling of being watched. At the back of her mind, in a place she did not notice, a voice said, "You dig or die."

***

By noon, the electricity returned, and the house began to creak. The old wood expanded and sighed in the heat. Somewhere in the walls, water kept dripping.

Drip.

Pause.

Drip.

That rhythm again — steady as a heartbeat.

She tried to drown it out with the radio, but every station played the same static hiss, a water-logged whisper beneath the white noise. At first, it sounded like wind. Then words.

Clara... clay to blood... blood to debt... debt to clay.

She turned the dial until the voice disappeared, leaving the air unnaturally silent. Her reflection in the window looked pale, her eyes sunken with exhaustion. For a moment behind that reflection, she thought she saw someone else — a man standing by the treeline, head bowed, hands moving as if digging.

She blinked. The yard was silent and empty, with only the darkened rings of wet soil, as if the earth beneath were seeping upward.

***

Later that night, the dreams arrived.

She was waist-deep in red water. The moon reflected through the trees from a coin dropped into the mud. The thirteen jars floated nearby, turning slowly, their lids missing. Each one contained something pale and human — a hand, a face, and an eye opening.

At the water's edge, a figure waited — Ridgely Smith Crockett — the same man she'd seen in the old photograph from the archives Ephraim had shown her in the diner. Here, strangely, he was younger. Whole. His eyes reflected the moonlight like a polished brass bed.

You opened the door.

Clara tried to move, but the mud gripped her legs like fingers.

You woke what sleeps in debt.

"I didn't mean to," she said.

Blood remembers, girl. Yours, above all.

He raised his hand. Thirteen dark shapes rose from the water, swirling in the air like leaves. Jars, each spinning faster until the

54

noise turned into wind. When she covered her ears, she could still hear him beneath it, whispering:

When the thirteenth arrives, the river claims. The time has come to dig or die.

She woke up gasping, her sheets soaked with sweat. Despite nighttime temperatures still in the eighties, the air in the room was cold enough for her to see her breath.

"I need a glass of water."

The floorboards in the hall were slick. Not from leaking pipes — the water was rising from below, seeping through the cracks in the floor as if something were breathing upward.

As she stepped closer, the puddle trembled and split open — a circle forming in its center. For a moment, her reflection stared back, distorted and shivering. Then it changed. The face staring back was not hers.

Crockett looked up from the floor, his grin broad and wet.

Debt's due, Harlan. Dig or die.

The lightbulb above her flickered and then shattered. Darkness descended swiftly, thick and complete. Somewhere in the blackness, a low chuckle echoed, like the gurgle of a drowning man who had decided not to fight anymore.

***

The next morning, Ephraim Tate's truck crunched along the gravel drive. Clara greeted him on the porch, eyes hollow, mud drying on her bare feet.

He looked at her for a long moment, then spoke. "You saw him."

She nodded.

"I told you the land remembers," he said, shaking his index finger at her. "The jars weren't filled with gold alone."

55

Ephraim stopped himself, then looked away toward the rings, as if he'd already gone too far. He sat next to Clara on the porch.

"They were meant to hold something, child," he said. "That's what Crockett believed."

Clara swallowed. "How do I stop it?"

Ephraim's face hardened. "You don't stop something that's been here so long that the land itself fears it. You put it back where it belongs. You give it what it's owed."

She looked toward the field. The air above the thirteen rings shimmered in the sunlight like a heat mirage, faintly smelling of rain and iron.

"I think it's already here to collect."

***

That night, thunder rumbled again in the west. Somewhere beyond the ridge, the reservoir's floodgates moaned. The forecast called for "localized flooding."

But down in Buck Run, the ground was already shifting — not downhill, not toward the water.

Inward.

CHAPTER 12 — THE ADVISORY

THIS IS AN ADVISORY FROM THE NATIONAL
WEATHER SERVICE

Heavy rain is expected, with total accumulations of 2 to 4 inches.
Flooding is possible in low-lying areas.

Avoid standing water, which may be deeper than it appears and can sweep
a vehicle away.

By late morning, the sky over Buck Run was the color of wet
concrete. Culverts and ditches became shallow rivers, and the creek
crept over its banks, slowly settling into the low fields like molasses
in January.

The jobsite remained shut down.

Clara had checked her phone twice before leaving the
farmhouse, as if staring at the same unread email might change the
message. No new schedule. No "all clear." Just the same clipped
line from the foreman earlier that morning:

High water. Stay put. We'll reassess.

Stay put.

As if the farmhouse had been built for waiting.

She hadn't slept. Not really. Every time she drifted off, she fell
straight into the same half-dream where the field behind the house
was perfectly dry and eerily silent. The thirteen rings looked less
like disturbed dirt and more like impressions forced into the land,
like thumbprints lifted from a crime scene.

She'd wake with her heart racing, the taste of pennies in her
mouth, and the sense that if she listened hard enough, she'd hear
her name spoken somewhere beneath the floor.

So she drove.

Not because driving would fix anything. Not because the diner
would either. But because sitting in the farmhouse, with the world
watching her through rain-streaked windows, had begun to feel like
someone—or something—else deciding for her.

The Last Stop Diner parking lot was half empty, though that didn't mean much. It was rural Virginia, after all. A diner could look deserted and still have a full table of men inside, talking loud enough to make the windows hum.

Clara shut the truck door and stood for a second, her hand on the roof, letting the damp air settle on her skin. Everything smelled of soaked soil and motor oil.

She tried not to look toward the creek.

She tried not to think about jars.

Inside, the diner was warm and bright in a way that felt slightly off, like a set from a TV show—built for comfort, but not real. The ceiling fans turned lazily, stirring the smell of bacon grease, coffee, and lemon disinfectant. A few people sat in booths—an older couple splitting a plate, two men in work shirts with mud on their boots, and a woman with a toddler, feeding him fries one by one like offerings to a bird.

Clara slid into a booth near the back, neither fully hidden nor in the open.

She didn't come here to see Wydra.

Not at first.

She came for the noise, for a place where the walls didn't creak as if they were speaking. She came for the illusion that the world still ran on ordinary things—breakfast orders, weather complaints, or someone asking for more creamer.

But the moment she sat down, she felt it anyway.

The same feeling she'd had the first time she walked in: that she was known here. Not in a friendly, small-town way. In a way that made her shoulders draw up before she knew why.

She rolled them once, like she could shake it off.

Wydra appeared at her table with a coffee pot in one hand, a pad in the other.

She wore the same uniform Clara remembered—black apron, hair pulled back, mouth neutral as if she'd practiced not reacting.

Her eyes flicked over Clara's face, then away, as if checking a label on a jar.

Wydra poured without asking, as if she didn't care whether Clara wanted coffee or not. The coffee was dark and steaming— the kind that kept you awake and made you feel worse later.

"Food?" Wydra asked.

Clara stared at the menu without seeing it. Her stomach felt hollow and knotted.

"Just... toast," she finally said. "And eggs."

Wydra wrote it down. Her pen scratched once, hard, as if the paper irritated her.

"You look like you haven't slept," Wydra said.

Clara forced a small laugh, but it came out thin. "I didn't."

Wydra's eyes lifted, sizing Clara up the way you might assess the weather. "That place'll do that."

Clara rubbed her eyes. "The farmhouse?"

Wydra gave the smallest shrug. "The land around here. It don't let everybody rest."

It should've sounded like a superstition, the kind of line you could dismiss with a smile.

But Wydra said it as if she were commenting on humidity.

Clara swallowed. "It's probably just stress."

Wydra looked at her for a moment, expression unchanged. "Sure."

Then she turned to go.

Clara watched her move through the diner, stop at another table, and smile—not a big smile, but a practiced one, part of the job. It was strange how quickly she could put it on and take it off.

Clara took a sip of coffee. It tasted like heat, bitterness, and being awake against your will.

She tried to focus on the jobsite. On the high water. On emails, schedules, and rational problems with rational fixes.

But her mind kept slipping sideways.

The thirteen rings.

The jars cracking.

Her grandfather's desk, the folder, the torn pages stitched together by silence.

The crazy rhymes that ran through her head.

And Ephraim—the old man who'd been sitting at the counter days ago, looking at her as if he'd been waiting.

She hadn't been sure what to make of him. There was something about him that felt like a warning disguised as a person.

She'd watched him, even if she hadn't admitted it to herself. The way people looked at him wasn't fear, exactly. It was that other thing. The quiet understanding that some men carried their own mysteries.

Clara had sat alone then, and he'd still found her.

You're blood to those who wronged Crockett.

Her fingers closed on the mug handle.

She wasn't gullible. She knew how stories grew in small towns—how grief, boredom, and old land could lead people to invent explanations and fill the gaps where facts didn't fit.

Still, some quiet, primal part of her kept remembering how the air had felt when she tried to step off the porch with the jars in her mind.

Humid. Humming. Listening.

Wydra returned with the toast and eggs, then set the plate down with a soft clink.

Clara forced herself to eat. The toast was buttered, and the eggs were hot, but she tasted almost nothing.

Wydra topped off her coffee without being asked.

Clara hesitated, then said carefully, "Can I ask you something?"

Wydra's hand paused above the pot. "You can ask."

Clara took a breath. "The man I talked to the other day, Ephraim."

Wydra's mouth didn't move, but something in her eyes did. A faint sharpening. A narrowing.

"What about him?" she asked.

Clara tried to keep her tone light. "He said some… things. About the land. About my grandfather."

Wydra set the coffee pot down on the table as if it had grown heavy.

"And you listened?"

"I didn't take it as fact," Clara said. "I just—he knew my name. He knew my family. He said my grandfather came here."

"He did," Wydra said. Her gaze slid toward the front windows and the gray daylight beyond them. "A couple of times a week, back when he could still drive himself. Same booth. Same order."

Clara's throat tensed. Her grandfather had never mentioned coming here, but he hadn't mentioned a lot of things, had he?

"What did he—" Clara started, then stopped. She didn't want to sound like she was interrogating. She didn't want to show how hungry she was for anything that made sense.

Wydra leaned a fraction closer, voice lower—not conspiratorial, just quieter.

"You ought to be careful around Ephraim," she said.

Clara's brow furrowed. "Why?"

Wydra's expression remained calm. "Because he likes to talk."

Clara almost smiled. "That's all?"

Wydra's eyes flicked back to her. "He likes to talk about things that don't concern him."

Clara felt her pulse kick. "What things?"

Wydra straightened, and the practiced waitress returned—chin level, hands busy. "He's been living here a long time. Long enough to mistake his own thoughts for truths."

Clara set her fork down. "So you're saying he's unreliable?"

"He ain't a preacher or a historian," Wydra said. "He's a man who listens long enough to think a story belongs to him, and he decides what it means."

Clara let that sit for a second because it was almost comforting. A rational explanation. A human one.

61

But then Wydra added softly, "And he ain't always wrong."

Clara's stomach tightened.

She looked up at Wydra. "Do you know anything about what he was talking about?"

Wydra's gaze didn't flicker. "No."

The word was clean and immediate. It hit the table like a judge's gavel.

Clara tried again from a different angle. "He said my grandfather asked for help with something."

Wydra picked up an empty plate from the neighboring booth, even though no one had asked her to. "Did he?"

Clara heard it—the shift. The dismissal beginning.

"He implied," Clara said, "that my grandfather wanted him to dig something up."

Wydra's mouth curved—not a smile. More like a grim acknowledgment that different people could repeat the same mistakes.

"Your grandfather was an old man," she said. "Old men get ideas."

Clara's frustration rose, quick and hot. "He wasn't irrational."

Wydra's eyes cut to hers. "You sure about that?"

Clara stiffened. "Yes."

Wydra looked at her for a long moment, and Clara had the sudden urge to explain herself—to defend her grandfather as if he could still hear it.

Wydra's voice stayed even. "Honey, you come in here and ask me if I know about whatever story Ephraim told you, and then you get mad when I don't agree with it."

"I'm not mad," Clara said too quickly.

Wydra raised an eyebrow. "You're tired. And you're scared. And you're standing on land that's been here a lot longer than you've been alive, thinkin' you can look it in the face and ask it questions like it owes you answers."

Clara's cheeks flushed. "That's not what I'm doing."

Wydra nodded, as if indulging her. "Right."

Clara leaned forward, lowering her voice now—not because she wanted secrecy, but because she didn't want the diner to hear her say the words out loud.

"My grandfather... did he ever mention anything strange to you?" she asked. "Anything he was worried about? Anything he was trying to fix?"

Wydra stared at her.

The air between them felt still, as if the diner had a switch and someone turned down the volume.

"No," Wydra said again. "He didn't."

Clara's jaw set. "He came here twice a week and never said a word."

Wydra shrugged. "Some folks don't run their mouths."

Clara exhaled, fighting the urge to push harder—and the sense she was being treated like a child, the way Wydra had treated her the first time, as if Clara's presence were a nuisance and her questions a game.

She softened her tone and tried to sound reasonable. "I'm just trying to understand what's happening out there," she said. "The jobsite is shut down. The creek is flooding. The soil—"

Wydra's eyes narrowed.

Clara stopped herself. She almost said *the jars*. She felt the words catch in her throat.

Wydra watched her anyway, as if she'd heard them.

Clara swallowed. "I don't want to make a mistake or ignore something I shouldn't."

Wydra's voice turned cool. "Then don't make one."

Clara blinked. "That's not—"

Wydra cut in, polite again in the way a door is polite when it closes. "Eat your eggs."

She lowered her gaze to the plate, stabbed at the eggs with her fork, but she didn't eat.

"Did you know my grandfather well?" Clara asked quietly.

Wydra looked down at the table, as if considering whether it was worth answering.

"I served him," she said.

"That's not the same thing."

Wydra's eyes lifted. "It's enough."

Clara tried one last approach, indirect and careful, like stepping around a sleeping animal.

"He kept things," Clara said. "Old things. Papers. Notes. He didn't talk about them much. But he… he didn't let go of certain parts of the past."

Wydra's expression didn't change.

Clara continued gently, "If he ever said anything here—anything about being afraid or trying to—"

Wydra leaned in, just slightly. Her voice dropped low enough that Clara had to strain to hear.

"Don't," she said.

The single word hit harder than the earlier "no."

Clara went still.

Wydra's eyes stayed locked on hers. Not threatening. Not kind. Simply fixed.

"Don't what?" Clara asked.

Wydra's mouth tightened as if she'd already given away too much. She straightened again, stepping back into her apron and her role.

"Don't turn Ephraim into an excuse," she said. "If you're lookin' for someone to tell you the world is simple again, you won't find it at this table."

Clara's voice came out rougher than she'd intended. "So you do know something."

Wydra stared at her, and for the first time, the mask slipped—not entirely, but enough.

"What I know," Wydra said, "is that grown women don't go chasin' half-drunken stories because they're bored."

Clara flinched. "I'm not bored."

Wydra's eyes flicked over Clara's face again. "No," she said. "You're lonely."

Clara's stomach dropped.

Wydra continued, almost casually, "And you're angry. You're angry at him for dyin' with his mouth shut and leavin' you to clean up what he didn't finish."

Clara's hand closed around the fork. "How would you—"

Wydra turned away as if she hadn't said anything unusual at all. "You want more coffee?"

Clara stared at her. "How would you know that?"

Wydra paused, her back half-turned, coffee pot in hand.

For a heartbeat, she didn't answer. The diner's noise filled the space—forks clinked against plates, someone laughed too loudly, the ceiling fan hummed.

Then Wydra said, without looking at Clara, "Because he used to sit right there, stirring his coffee until it went cold, and he'd talk about you as if you were a storm he could see coming and couldn't stop."

Clara's throat tightened.

"My grandfather talked about me?" she whispered.

Wydra finally glanced back, her expression flat again, as if she regretted the sentence the moment it was spoken.

"He talked about you," she said. "And he talked about what you'd do with the land."

Clara's heart thudded.

"What did he say?" Clara asked.

Wydra's mouth formed a small, dismissive line, and she picked up the coffee pot again as if it gave her something to do with her hands.

"He said," Wydra replied, "that you'd go diggin'."

Clara went very still.

Wydra leaned in just enough for Clara to hear her next words over the diner's noise.

"And he said," Wydra added, "you'd think you were the first Harlan to do it."

Then she straightened, poured coffee into Clara's mug as if nothing had happened, and walked away.

Clara sat very still until she realized she hadn't moved since Wydra walked away.

The coffee had turned cold before she noticed.

CHAPTER 13 — THE CREEK

Wydra left the diner by the back door.

The rain had intensified while she worked the tables—not a hard storm, something worse. An unrelenting bombardment of water that made the parking lot swim and kept the world the color of quarried granite. The gravel out back had turned to paste. The air smelled like the fur of a wet dog, with something faintly metallic that didn't belong.

She didn't hurry.

Wydra moved the way she always did, as if time were a tool she carried in her apron pocket—something she decided when to use. She crossed a narrow strip of grass and followed the service road until the neon glow of the diner disappeared behind the trees.

The land dipped toward Buck Run, toward the hollow, toward the place where water refused to obey the rules.

She kept her hands in her coat pockets. Coins pressed cold against her fingers.

When she reached the creek, she stopped at the same spot she always chose—the bank that softened underfoot even when summer baked everything else to dust. A place where the ground stayed willing.

Wydra knelt.

She pressed the first coin into the mud.

It disappeared without a sound, as if the earth had opened its mouth and closed it again.

The second coin took longer. The mud resisted, then yielded with a faint suction pop that made her ears ache.

By the third, the creek began to change.

Not rising. Not flooding.

Listening.

The water shivered in small, tight ripples. Bubbles surfaced and popped with soft hisses, like breath that had been held too long.

Wydra stood.

The mud near the bank thickened and rolled, not like something boiling, but like something turning over in its sleep.

Ridgely rose slowly.

First, a shoulder slick with black mud. Then an arm. Then his head bowed, as if the weight of the ground still pressed on his neck. When he straightened, it was only because the land allowed it.

He did not look like a man rescued from drowning.

He looked like a man who had stopped fearing it.

His eyes lifted at last, dull at first—then sharpening, as if the act of being called dragged his mind into focus, whether he wanted it or not.

"You're feeding it heavy tonight."

Wydra's expression didn't change. "You've been bleeding through."

Ridgely's mouth tightened. Water dripped from his sleeves and sank into the bank as if the ground drank it.

"She's already awake."

Wydra's voice stayed calm. "She's tired."

"She's listening."

"She shouldn't be."

Ridgely laughed softly, and the sound was wrong—thin and wet, like it had to travel through mud in his throat to reach the air.

"You think you can keep it quiet by pretending it isn't there," he said.

Wydra stepped closer to the edge of the bank. Her boots sank slightly, the earth accommodating her as if it recognized one of its own.

"You know the terms," she said.

Ridgely's gaze dropped to the creek, to the bubbles still popping in the shallows.

"I know the pain," he said. "I know how it felt to stop breathing."

His eyes lifted again.

"I didn't know you," he added.

Wydra's fingers tightened in her pocket around the remaining coins.

"You chose," she said.

Ridgely's head tilted a fraction. "I answered a voice that used my brother's name."

The creek babbled once, as if amused.

Wydra did not react. She didn't give him the satisfaction of naming what had happened aloud.

"You've been pushing," she said. "Testing. Letting her feel you under that house."

Ridgely's eyes narrowed. "Under her house," he corrected.

Wydra ignored the correction. "You let her see you. Hear you. Smell you."

"She opened what was sealed," Ridgely said. "She didn't do it on purpose, but she did it."

"She doesn't understand where she's standing," Wydra replied.

Ridgely's face shifted at that. Not in triumph or anger.

It was something worse.

Hope.

"She's the last," he said.

Wydra's eyes hardened. "Don't speak about her like she's a key."

Ridgely's gaze flicked toward the dark line of trees, toward the higher ground where the farmhouse sat unseen.

"I don't need to speak her name," he said. "The land already knows it."

Wydra took one slow breath.

This was the first time his voice had carried that way—not pleading, not threatening, but certain.

"You think she can free you?" Wydra said.

Ridgely didn't answer at first. The creek moved around his boots, warm and slow, circling as if it couldn't decide whether he belonged above or below the water.

Then he said, "She can end it."

Wydra's mouth turned faintly downward. Not a frown. Something colder. Calculation.

"And if she ends it," Wydra said, "what happens to me?"

Ridgely met her eyes.

For the first time, he looked less like a story told to scare children and more like a man trapped in a prison sentence.

"I don't care," he said.

Wydra nodded, as if that was the expected answer.

"You're still bound to what I did... and you don't get to decide where the consequences stop."

Ridgely's shoulders sagged slightly, as if the word *peace* hurt his ears.

"You've had years you didn't earn," he said.

"And you've had years you didn't die," Wydra replied, still and watchful. "We both got what we needed."

Ridgely's laugh this time was quieter. Almost human.

"You're worried," he said.

Wydra didn't blink. "I'm aware."

"Of her," he said.

Wydra's hand slid deeper into her pocket, touching the coins again, grounding herself in their weight.

"I'm aware," she repeated, "that you are forgetting your place."

Ridgely looked down at his boots, at the mud sucking lightly around them, patient and possessive.

"My place," he said, "is a grave that never rests."

Wydra stepped closer.

The creek responded. The water thickened. The mud at Ridgely's feet tightened as if it took direction from her.

"You will not reach for her again," Wydra said.

Ridgely's eyes lifted. The hope didn't leave them. It stayed, stubborn as a bruise.

"I don't have to," he said. "She's already reaching."

That was the shift.

Not a threat. Not a spell.

A fact.

Wydra knelt, pulled the coins from her pocket, and pressed them into the mud one after another—methodical, practiced, as if she'd done this more times than she wanted to remember.

The creek surged, slapping the bank.

Ridgely's body sank an inch.

Then another.

The mud climbed him, slow and twining.

He did not thrash. He did not beg.

His breath hitched once, caught between relief and grief.

"You will stay," Wydra said. "And you will keep quiet."

Ridgely looked at her as the mud rose to his ribs.

"You can't put it back," he said softly. "Not all the way."

Wydra's voice remained even. "Watch me."

The mud climbed to his chest, his throat.

His eyes stayed on hers.

"She's going to choose," Ridgely said, and his voice was steadier than it had any right to be.

The creek swallowed the last of him.

The water smoothed. The bubbles faded. The bank settled back into ordinary mud, as if the earth hadn't just taken a man.

Wydra stood alone in the rain.

The coins were gone from her hand, and the emptiness they left behind felt like an accounting error.

She looked toward the dark trees on the rise, toward the unseen house beyond them, not with fear—never fear.

With resolve.

With ownership.

With the kind of determination that comes from someone who has stolen time and refuses to give it back.

Wydra turned and walked away from the creek, already thinking of what would need to be reinforced—what would need to be watched—what would need to be kept from a tired woman in a farmhouse who didn't yet know she had power.

Behind her, Buck Run flowed on.

And for the first time in a long time, something beneath it had hope.

CHAPTER 14 — THE FLOOD

The fury of the nor'easter arrived at dusk. Clara knew the waiting was over.

First, the air went still, as it does before a siren sounds — a silence that blanketed the world. Then the wind came, pulling the smell of mud and rain up from the hollow. The trees on the ridge bent until their tops touched, their branches rattling like bones.

At Buck Run, a mile from the farmhouse, the creek had risen into a brown, twisting vein cutting straight through the field.

Lightning tore across the sky. For a moment, the entire valley was bathed in white light — the kind that etched itself into your eyes. When it dimmed, something else moved through the rain.

A man's shape, waist-deep in the floodwater.

Then, many shapes. Thirteen shadows swayed from head to knees, mouths open in the same silent scream.

Meanwhile, Clara stood on the porch, watching the first wave of rain creep across the pasture.

The rings in the soil had vanished — drowned.

Her phone buzzed once before losing service.

A text from an unknown number.

"Don't go outside. It's awake."

***

By midnight, the house groaned with water.
The crawl-space hatch bulged upward, and each wave of water produced a dull thud from beneath the floorboards.

Clara gathered what she could — a lantern, boots, her grandfather's *Bible*, and the old map Ephraim had given her. The ink was bleeding, and the mark of thirteen jars blurred into one dark stain.

73

Outside, the wind screamed through the trees. The air smelled wrong — not rain, not rot. It smelled of metal and blood.

When the power line blew in the yard, the light that appeared wasn't electricity. It was something older, white as bone, flickering across the wires like heartbeats on a monitor struggling to hold a pulse.

And then she heard it again — the voice that had haunted every Harlan since the night of the robbery:

Clara...

Debt to blood... blood to clay... clay to river...
Bring me home.

The words felt rehearsed, as if someone else had taught him how to say them.

At that moment, the floorboards split with a crack like a gunshot.

Water surged through the seams, black and foaming, carrying fragments of glass. Jars. Dozens. Hundreds. They clinked together, forming a ghastly chorus rising from the depths.

Clara stumbled backward, clutching the *Bible*. The room pulsed with heat and cold. The walls looked as if they were sweating. Every nail hissed.

The air filled with laughter — no longer human. It rolled beneath her feet, trembling the foundation.

Then he arrived.

Ridgely Smith Crockett stepped through the gap in the floor as if emerging from his own grave. His skin was like mud, and his eyes were twin lanterns of amber fire. Water streamed from his mouth as he spoke.

"Your blood has bought my prison, child. Now you'll bury me properly."

She could barely breathe. "What do you want from me?"

Even as she asked, Clara knew the answer would cost her the house.

"Rest. Or ruin. Dig or die. Your choice."

The *Bible* in her hands fluttered open — not to scripture but to a loose page slipped between the verses. Her grandfather's handwriting was scrawled there.

Thirteen jars. Thirteen debts. Speak the binding where the river meets the tree.

***

The door of the construction trailer ripped off its hinges.

The wind pushed Clara from her truck into a world of water and noise. Rain lashed sideways, stinging her face, and the field disappeared beneath the rising flood, churning with leaves and debris. She saw the sycamore ahead, its crown glowing white with lightning.

She ran.

Behind her, Crockett followed — his footsteps left no splash, only ripples that faintly glowed, each burning through the water like fire beneath oil.

The creek had swollen into something unrecognizable, a single, churning mass. The sycamore's roots were half-buried, slick and coiled. At their base, thirteen jars floated in a circle, bobbing like candles on a dark altar.

Clara waded in until the current reached her waist. Her lips trembled as she read from the page, the words caught between sobs and thunder.

"Earth to clay, debt repaid,
River take what man betrayed—"

Ridgely Smith Crockett roared. The sound split the air, and the flood surged around her. His hand rose — mud, bone, and light. It struck her in the chest, knocking the breath from her lungs. The *Bible* flew into the water.

She went under.

The current spun her around. The world dissolved into bubbles, mud, and darkness.

Somewhere in that blackness, the jars began to break.

Each one burst with a flash — not gold, but the memory of it — as a face dissolved into light.

When she surfaced, Crockett was screaming, his form unraveling in the torrent.

From his chest spilled not blood but water, rushing out in a glowing cascade against the night.

Thirteen for sin… thirteen for blood… His voice broke, then faded into the wind.

Debt forgiven.

He fell backward as the current swept him away. The light left his eyes.

***

The storm peaked, then broke.

By dawn, the water had receded almost as quickly as it had risen. Buck Run steamed beneath a sky so clear it hurt to look at. The trailer was half-collapsed, and the fields were scoured flat.

Only the sycamore remained untouched, its roots washed bare and gleaming.

As if it had always been waiting.

Clara crawled from the mud, coughing up river water, her hands trembling. At the base of the tree, one jar remained untouched.

Inside, the last of Ridgely Smith Crockett's gold gleamed beside something pale and small.

A magnolia petal, pressed flat and intact.

She knelt, touched the glass, and whispered, "Rest."

The jar's light dimmed.

The creek's laughter faded.

CHAPTER 15 — THE THIRTEENTH JAR

By noon, the sky had burned clear.

Mist rose from the fields in slow ribbons, blurring the edges of the world. The air carried the strange sweetness left behind after a flood — silt, sap, and something faintly metallic, like blood remembered.

Clara sat in the mud at the base of the sycamore.

Her arms ached, and her breathing was shallow and ragged.

All around her lay the remains of the jars — shards of glass glinting in the light, each holding a tiny pool of water. The creek whispered nearby, calm again, its voice soft and almost apologetic.

Only one jar remained intact.

It sat upright among the roots, its glass dulled by silt. Inside, the last coin glistened faintly beside the pressed magnolia petal, still whole after all those years.

She lifted it carefully. The water inside pulsed once, faintly — a tiny heartbeat. Then the light began to fade.

Rest.

The word did not come from the air or from any voice outside her, but from somewhere deep within — soft, resigned, grateful.

She dug a shallow hole between the roots with her bare hands. The clay was cool and slick, clinging to her fingers as if reluctant to let go. She set the jar inside and pressed it down until the water completely covered it.

The earth trembled, not violently but as a long exhale — and then went still.

As the water smoothed and the last light faded from the glass, Clara found herself thinking not of Ridgely Smith Crockett but of Wydra. Of how some wrongs are bound because they are named, while others linger because no one ever claimed them.

Ridgely could rest now — his debt spoken aloud, his suffering answered. There was no one left to pass the land to, no one waiting for it to change hands. But Wydra's had never been. The land was quiet — but quiet was not the same as safe.

Clara understood then that what had been broken here could be broken again, given the wrong hands and the wrong hunger. She pressed the soil firmly over the jar, not in fear but in resolve, and stayed where she was long after the creek fell silent.

Wydra Grace was gone, her fate unknown — and Clara knew that what vanished without reckoning could return one day.

The rain returned, this time gently, rinsing the silt from her arms and face. When she looked up, sunlight broke through the clouds. For the first time since she'd come back, the light did not feel harsh.

It felt earned. It felt like a release.

***

She made her way back to what remained of the farmhouse. Half the roof had collapsed, and the porch had fallen into the foundation. Yet the air inside was dry, and the smell of iron had gone.

Stepping inside, clutching her grandfather's *Bible* she'd found floating in Buck Run, she noticed a loose page still folded between the Psalms. The ink had smudged, but one line was legible.

Some debts are written in the ground, and only the ground can erase them.

She pressed the paper against the wall to dry, then stepped back into the light.

CHAPTER 16 — AFTERMATH

Two weeks later, heavy equipment rumbled up the access road.

The data company sent engineers and surveyors to assess the damage. They spent hours walking the property, driving stakes into the soft clay, and taking readings.

Temporary lights installed at the jobsite shone across the field like fireflies.

Clara watched from the ridge.

When they left, she found one of their reports snagged on the wire fence.

SITE NOT SUITABLE FOR DEVELOPMENT

Unstable subsurface conditions. Persistent moisture of unknown origin.

She smiled. "Good."

The paper shivered in the breeze, tore loose, then spun toward the creek.

That evening, as the sun set behind the ridge, she returned to the sycamore. The ground there was firm again, though darker than the rest of the field, richer, almost black. Wildflowers had already begun to push through the churned soil: blue vervain, spiderwort, and a few early asters.

She sat with her back against the tree, closing her eyes. The wind moved through the branches, carrying the faint scent of rain and old wood. Somewhere below, the creek whispered, not in laughter but in song — the sound of water over smooth stone.

For the first time, she no longer heard laughter. Only breath. Only peace.

She reached into her pocket and found a coin she hadn't realized she still had, dull and green, stamped with the letters R. S. C. She turned it once in her fingers, then threw it into the water. It made barely a sound, sank quickly, and vanished in a trail of silver bubbles.

When she looked up, the sun reflected perfectly off the ripples. For a moment, the entire creek seemed to glow from within, as if the land itself had taken a long, contented breath and finally, finally let it out.

Autumn came slowly. The county declared Buck Run "environmentally unstable." Official language, clean and bloodless. The data center project vanished without announcement. The survey flags came down, and the access road grew over with broom sedge and vines.

FEMA workers came and went, taking photos and measurements. They left politely but quickly, uneasy in the dim light. None of them stayed past sunset. Every night, as the sun dipped behind the ridge, the fog returned — a slow, low tide creeping out of the creek. It wasn't threatening anymore, just there, like breath on a cold morning.

***

Clara stayed to clean up what remained of the farmhouse.

Ephraim Tate arrived one Sunday afternoon, his old Ford crunching over gravel. He found Clara in the yard, kneeling by the foundation, pulling ivy from the stones.

He leaned on his cane. "You look better."

She offered a faint smile. "I am sleeping now."

He nodded, glancing toward Buck Run.

"You did what no one else could."

Clara brushed dirt from her hands.

"I didn't," she said. "I just listened."

Ephraim smiled faintly. "That's what I mean. I didn't know it was meant for you until it was done. Some things only make sense afterward."

"You could have tried," she said.

"I wasn't meant to," he replied simply.

He opened his truck door and paused. "You keeping the property?"

"For now. Maybe plant wildflowers. Maybe do nothing. Some places aren't meant to be changed."

He nodded again, his eyes bright. "That'll do."

When he drove away, the road swallowed his dust.

That night, the wind swept down from the Blue Ridge mountains, bringing the first real chill of the season. The sycamore's leaves trembled, rustling softly, almost like voices. Clara stood on the porch and watched fog rise again from the hollow, slow and silver under the moon.

It reached the base of the house, curled around the steps, and stopped there — like a dog come to lie at her feet. For the first time, she didn't step back.

"Goodnight," she said softly.

And the fog, as if understanding, rolled back toward the creek.

CHAPTER 17 — THE HOLLOW SLEEPS

Winter settled in gently. Snow fell early, soft as ash, muffling the woods in a stillness so deep it felt sacred. The field lay smooth again, no rings, no scars.

Only the sycamore stood as a witness, bare-limbed and watchful.

Clara built a small cabin near the ridge from salvaged wood, just high enough to see the valley below. The house that had once stood on her grandfather's land was gone. She didn't rebuild it. Some things, she knew now, weren't meant to rise again.

She kept busy throughout the winter with small things: Planting seeds. Writing letters. Drinking coffee on the porch as the fog lifted each morning.

Every so often, she thought she heard laughter down in the hollow, but it wasn't cruel anymore.

It was content, the sound of water smoothing stones.

The *Culpeper Star-Exponent* published a brief piece in February.
DATA CENTER RELOCATION APPROVED
Project to Move to Prince William County Amid "Site Instability" Issues

No mention of Buck Run.

She folded the article and slipped it into her grandfather's *Bible*, next to the blurred verse that once guided her through the storm.

***

In spring, she returned to the sycamore. Wildflowers had overtaken the hollow in a burst of color, blues, purples, and pale white blossoms clustering around the roots like candles. The ground was dry, and the air was warm. The creek flowed clear for the first time in generations.

The hollow slept now, not because it was finished, but because someone was still listening. She knelt and touched the earth. It felt cool and alive.

"Rest easy," she whispered.

Something in the breeze shifted — not a word, not even a sound, just a faint sign of gratitude. A sigh deep in the roots.

She turned back toward the ridge. Sunlight struck the water, and for a moment the reflection took on the shape of a face — young, peaceful, eyes closed.

Then the ripples carried it away.

The hollow was quiet once more. Not the silence of death or fear — but of sleep.

ABOUT THE AUTHOR

Books by J.D. Toepfer

Route 666

Sins of the Fathers

The Gathering Storm

Evil Reigns

John "J.D." Toepfer is the award-winning author of the *Highway to Hell* series, a supernatural saga blending historical mystery, occult intrigue, and apocalyptic horror. *Literary Titan* describes the series as "suspenseful horror that gives readers bits of historical information, occult, and the supernatural, all combined into a thrilling read."

When he isn't exploring the darker corners of human choice and consequence, J.D. can often be found working in his garden, where many of his most unexpected plot twists first take root.

Visit www.jdtoepfer.com for updates on upcoming releases.

Acknowledgments:

My wife, Christina, whose unwavering support and encouragement make all of this possible. I love you more than I can say.

My brother, George, who has always been my first editor and a large part of everything I do. This would be no fun without you.

My readers and fans… where would I be without your support? Thank you for traveling the Highway to Hell with me.

Made in the USA
Monee, IL
07 July 2026

56550193R00052